THE MURDER PACT

M A COMLEY

JEAMEL PUBLISHING LIMITED

New York Times and USA Today bestselling author M A Comley
Published by Jeamel Publishing limited
Copyright © 2019 M A Comley
Digital Edition, License Notes

This is a work of fiction. Names, characters, places and incidents are a product of the author's imagination or are used fictitiously, and any resemblance to actual persons living or dead, business establishments, events or locales is entirely coincidental.

OTHER BOOKS BY M A COMLEY

Blind Justice (Novella)

Cruel Justice (Book #1)

Mortal Justice (Novella)

Impeding Justice (Book #2)

Final Justice (Book #3)

Foul Justice (Book #4)

Guaranteed Justice (Book #5)

Ultimate Justice (Book #6)

Virtual Justice (Book #7)

Hostile Justice (Book #8)

Tortured Justice (Book #9)

Rough Justice (Book #10)

Dubious Justice (Book #11)

Calculated Justice (Book #12)

Twisted Justice (Book #13)

Justice at Christmas (Short Story)

Prime Justice (Book #14)

Heroic Justice (Book #15)

Shameful Justice (Book #16)

Immoral Justice (Book #17)

Toxic Justice (Book #18)

Overdue Justice (Book #19)

Unfair Justice (a 10,000 word short story)

Irrational Justice (a 10,000 word short story)

Seeking Justice (a 15,000 word novella)

Caring For Justice (a 24,000 word novella)

Clever Deception (co-written by Linda S Prather)

Tragic Deception (co-written by Linda S Prather)

Sinful Deception (co-written by Linda S Prather)

Forever Watching You (DI Miranda Carr thriller)

Wrong Place (DI Sally Parker thriller #1)

No Hiding Place (DI Sally Parker thriller #2)

Cold Case (DI Sally Parker thriller#3)

Deadly Encounter (DI Sally Parker thriller #4)

Lost Innocence (DI Sally Parker thriller #5)

Web of Deceit (DI Sally Parker Novella with Tara Lyons)

The Missing Children (DI Kayli Bright #1)

Killer On The Run (DI Kayli Bright #2)

Hidden Agenda (DI Kayli Bright #3)

Murderous Betrayal (Kayli Bright #4)

Dying Breath (Kayli Bright #5)

The Hostage Takers (DI Kayli Bright Novella)

No Right to Kill (DI Sara Ramsey #1)

Killer Blow (DI Sara Ramsey #2)

The Dead Can't Speak (DI Sara Ramsey #3)

Deluded (DI Sara Ramsey #4)

The Murder Pact (DI Sara Ramsey #5)

The Caller (co-written with Tara Lyons)

Evil In Disguise – a novel based on True events

Deadly Act (Hero series novella)

Torn Apart (Hero series #1)

End Result (Hero series #2)

In Plain Sight (Hero Series #3)

Double Jeopardy (Hero Series #4)

Sole Intention (Intention series #1)

Grave Intention (Intention series #2)

Devious Intention (Intention #3)

The Man In The House (co-authored with Emmy Ellis)

The Lady In The Street (co-authored with Emmy Ellis)

The Child In The Tree (co-authored with Emmy Ellis)

Merry Widow (A Lorne Simpkins short story)

It's A Dog's Life (A Lorne Simpkins short story)

A Time To Heal (A Sweet Romance)

A Time For Change (A Sweet Romance)

High Spirits

The Temptation series (Romantic Suspense/New Adult Novellas)

Past Temptation

Lost Temptation

Tempting Christa (co-authored with Tracie Delaney) Billionaire romantic suspense series #1

Avenging Christa (co-authored with Tracie Delaney) Billionaire romantic suspense series #2

KEEP IN TOUCH WITH THE AUTHOR:

Newsletter
http://smarturl.it/8jtcvv

BookBub
www.bookbub.com/authors/m-a-comley

Blog
http://melcomley.blogspot.com

ACKNOWLEDGMENTS

Thank you as always to my rock, Jean, I'd be lost without you in my life.

Special thanks as always go to @studioenp for their superb cover design expertise.

My heartfelt thanks go to my wonderful editor Emmy Ellis, my proofreaders Joseph, Barbara and Jacqueline for spotting all the lingering nits.

A special shoutout to all the wonderful Bloggers and Facebook groups for their never-ending support of my work.

A GOOD friend would bail you out of jail…
While a BEST friend will be the one sitting next to you saying, 'damn
that was awesome'. Author unknown.

To Jacqueline, Mie, Maria, Di and Keely, true friends in every respect.
Thank you for allowing me to use your names in this book…don't go
getting any ideas now, ladies, remember it's fiction. 😊

PROLOGUE

The night was drawing in. She would be shielded by the darkness. There he was now.

Her heart raced, thundering against her ribs so hard it took her breath away. Now a dilemma ran through her mind: was she up to this? Would she be able to pull this off? She had to. There was no backing out now, it had all been agreed.

She watched him secure the gates and then made her move. Withdrawing the gun from her pocket, she closed the gap between them and jabbed the nose of the barrel in his back. "Do as I say, and you won't get hurt." It was a lie, but he wasn't to know that.

"What? Who are you? What do you want?"

"Shut up! Just shut your mouth. Over there." She pointed at the trail beside his business which led to the river.

"Why? It's dark down there, no streetlights."

"Doh! That's the idea, big man."

She smiled beneath her mask, her voice sounding gravelly, disguised in case he recognised it. Even if he did, it wouldn't matter, not in a few minutes.

"Why are you doing this?" His steps faltered slightly and there was evidence of panic in his tone, probably fearing what was about to happen.

Good, it was right for him to fear her. She had the power in her hands whether to strip his life away or to let him live. Tonight, it had been decided: his life would end. First, she intended to make him suffer. Humiliation was the key to her revenge.

"Ouch! I can't see a damn thing," he complained, stubbing his toe on an exposed stone prominently jutting out in the path.

"That's half the fun, isn't it? Scrabbling around in the dark; isn't that how you prefer to do things? Didn't you grope that young lady in the dark? Thought you'd got away with it, too, didn't you? *Wrong*."

"I don't know what you're talking about," he blustered, trying to twist to face her.

She jabbed the gun harder into his back. "Keep going. Turn around, and I'll shoot."

"What's this all about? Why are you doing this to me? You're mistaken if you think I've done something wrong."

She laughed, cautiously disguising the noise because he knew her laugh. He'd always ribbed her about her mimicking a donkey when she let loose. "I'll give you this, you're a trier. You're also a goddamn liar, and a cheating bastard to boot."

He tried to turn and face her again. She'd had enough and tapped him on the back of the head with the gun.

"Ouch! Don't hurt me, please don't hurt me. I have a wife and a child. They're reliant on me. My wife doesn't work. If you kill me, who will look after them?"

She paused, hesitating as she thought. Then, as it dawned on her, she prodded him in the back and ordered, "Less chat and more movement."

"Please, you don't understand. My wife is useless. I don't mean that disrespectfully. Oh damn, the words are coming out all wrong. She needs me, she's dependent on me, she doesn't have a clue how to exist without me. It's true, I'm not having you on. Please, I'm begging you to reconsider, for my family's sake."

"They'll be better off without you," she mumbled, not expecting him to hear her.

"They won't," he screeched, stopping to face her.

"Turn the other way and walk. Don't make me do something that I'll regret."

"Please, I have money. I'll give you a million pounds, more if you want it."

She snorted. "Ha, that's your answer for everything, isn't it? To pay someone off. Isn't that what happened to the girl you groped?"

"I…how do you know about that?"

"I know everything. All your dark, murky secrets. There's nothing I don't know about your shady past. The secrets you tried to keep from your wife. You're as stupid as you look. You've taken her for granted for too many years now. She's guilty of accepting it as a way of life for too long. Now, she's had enough. We've *all* had enough. This is the end. Your end. You'll no longer be able to hurt her with your wandering eye and lecherous hands. Women deserve better than to stand next to you on tenterhooks, not knowing if you'll touch them in intimate places or not."

"I wholeheartedly dispute that. I have never laid a hand on anyone who didn't want me to touch them…" His voice trailed off as if he'd realised his mistake when she pressed the gun deeper into his back.

"Move. Stop spilling lies for a change. Every time you open your damn mouth another lie enters the world. Well, not for much longer."

They walked several more steps before she instructed him to stop. "Here will do fine. Now, get undressed."

He spun around, almost knocking the gun out of her hand. She hadn't expected that and chastised herself for being sloppy.

"Please, I'll do anything but undress. It's cold."

She laughed, knowing how this was going to pan out. *He'll feel a darn sight colder in a few minutes when he meets his fate.* "Stop trying to delay the inevitable. *Do it.*"

"I can't. I don't want to."

She had to think fast on her feet. She shrugged. "Okay, if you don't, I'll shoot you now, and when I leave here, I'm going to drive to

3

your house in Tupsley and shoot your wife, Mie, and your daughter, Lizzie. She's away at Newcastle University, isn't she? Ha! I know all that needs to be known about your family and more. For instance, I know how much Mie despises you—she has done for years. Sex has consisted of her lying back and thinking of England—yes, I know she's Danish, but she's adapted well over the years to the British way of life. She's told me how much you make her skin crawl, the way you touch her in bed at night. You see, nothing is sacred. I know what she thinks and how she wants to go ahead with her life, without you."

He gasped and attempted to grab the weapon.

She backed up out of his reach and lifted her arm, aiming the gun at his chest. "Do what I told you to do and strip."

"And if I don't?"

She cocked the gun.

His hands swiftly got to work, shedding his clothes within seconds. He threw them aside and they landed in a heap on the grass verge alongside the path. Before long, he was standing naked in front of her. She eyed him up and down, his hands covering his shrivelled manhood. His body was toned for his age; he was forty-two, but then, men like him preferred to remain slim for when they went on the prowl for the next woman to bed.

He did nothing for her. No, that was wrong, he angered her. She felt nothing but hatred and disgust for the man who had brought shame on his family. He hadn't thought of the consequences when he'd groped that young woman. In cases such as this, it was often the family members who suffered the most, not the offender. Clearly, that was true here.

"Now what? It's cold."

"I want you to repent of your sins, all of them, and yes, I realise we could be here all night. If you don't want to freeze to death, I suggest you get on with it ASAP."

He shook his head. "I won't do it. I have nothing to say to you. Who the hell do you think you are?"

"Someone who holds the upper hand. You must be thicker than you look. Is it true?"

"What?"

"That men's brains are in their dicks?" She chortled; she couldn't help herself.

"No. I have brains in my head. I know, for instance, when someone has entered into doing something they may later regret, isn't that what this is all about? You thought this would be a good idea, and now, now, you're having second thoughts, isn't that the case? Otherwise, you would have shot me by now, true?"

It was, but she wasn't about to let on. Actually, his ballsy rhetoric had now placed yet another nail in his coffin. "Shut the fuck up, you know nothing. Turn around. I'd rather not see your ugly face. Some women might find you attractive, but over the years, your Scandinavian good looks have developed a hatred in me that I'm about to unleash."

"I'm sorry. My big mouth runs away from me at times. Truly, please, I'm sorry. Let's talk about this some more. Don't do anything rash, I'm begging you."

She glanced down at the ground beside her and strained to see through the darkness. Her eyes adjusted on the large stone lying off to her left. Keeping the fake gun aimed at Lens, she grabbed the stone and ran at him, bashing him hard on the back of his head. He went down quicker than a deflating balloon.

He stared up at her in shock. "Why? Don't do this, please. Think of Mie and Lizzie."

She raised her arm above her head and then dropped to her knees and bludgeoned his head with the stone over and over again, Mie's and Lizzie's faces uppermost in her mind.

"I'm doing this for their benefit, not mine. Rot in Hell, moron. The world will be a better place without you."

Once she'd witnessed the light fade in his eyes, she released the stone, stood, grabbed him by the ankles, dragged him to the water's edge and rolled him into the river. There was a five foot drop at this time of year. The water was low as they hadn't had much seasonal rain yet.

She retraced her steps and hunted for the stone for a few minutes.

In the darkness it was impossible to find. Damn, why hadn't she brought her mobile with her? Because she didn't want it to track her movements, that was why. With no torch to hand, the stone would have to wait. Thankfully, she had worn gloves, so there was no way his death could lead back to her.

One down, three to go. An excitement she never knew existed ran through her as she made her way back to her car which she'd parked a few streets away.

1

Sara Ramsey had that Monday-morning feeling, despite it being a Tuesday, when she drove into work that day. Carla was dashing from her car, the rain coming down in sheets as Sara pulled into the station car park.

She grabbed her bag from the front seat and darted across the tarmac to the main entrance, thankful that her designated space was closer to the station than most. "Bloody weather. Still, we shouldn't complain. It's been drier than normal for most of the year. How are you?"

Carla shrugged. "So-so. In dire need of a morning cup of coffee. How's your dad?"

"He's fine. I rang home last night and promised I'd call in on the way home. Mum sounded more cheerful than she has been in a while, so that's something to be grateful for. Did you see your fella last night?"

They walked up the stairs. Carla's cheeks turned a beetroot shade.

Sara elbowed her in the ribs. "Go on, fill me in on all the gruesome details."

Carla pulled a face and shook her head. "Go get your kinky thrills someplace else. My love life is private now, and in the future."

Sara paused on the steps and stared at her, mouth gaping for a second or two until she recovered. "What the fuck? Are you kidding me?"

"No. The relationship is still in its infancy, and I'm going to do all I can to keep it on the straight and narrow without any interference from you or anyone else."

What a strange comeback. Has someone said something they shouldn't have? What's her problem? It's a partner's right to prod and poke fun at her, isn't it?

"Ooo...get you. Someone got out of bed the wrong side this morning."

"I did *not*. Why is it when I want to keep a secret around here, I'm not allowed to? Can I just remind you that it took over eighteen months for you to tell us what had gone on in Manchester and the reason that brought you to Hereford?"

Sara shook her head. Obviously, the way Carla was reacting, Sara had touched a nerve. Maybe Carla and her fireman hunk had split up. Shit! She hoped not. Being with Gary Charlton had mellowed Carla over the past few months. Yes, she had her moments when she was tetchy about their dating, like today, but mostly, Carla had swanned around the office with a smilier face than normal, not that she was ever in a bad mood. "Can we start over? Unless there's something you want to get off that pert chest of yours."

Carla creased up. "Pert chest? Is that your way of telling me it's small?"

"No, not at all. Stop trying to put words into my mouth. Look, all I'm struggling to say is that my shoulder is always available if you need it to cry on."

"Thanks. There's no need, though. Everything is hunky-dory in the love life department."

"Now you're simply confusing me."

"Is that difficult?" Carla quipped, running ahead up the stairs.

Sara chased her and almost fell flat on her face when she messed up her stride on the final step. Luckily, she was holding on to the railing which helped keep her upright. "Damn heels, they'll be the death of me one day."

Carla waved her foot in front of her, lifting her trouser leg to reveal flat ankle boots in a dusty shade of pink. "You need to wear something like this, rather than those heels. What if we had to chase a suspect? I know I'd catch the bastard before you ever got going."

"You think pink boots are practical? I hope, for your sake, we don't get called out to a field full of cowpats today."

"You're so funny, not. As if that's likely to happen. They might not be the most practical colour to wear but at least they're comfortable."

"Whatever. Shall we see what overnight has brought our way?"

They were the first to arrive as usual, and Carla switched on the computer screens on all of her colleagues' desks then crossed the room to the vending machine.

Sara braced herself for what lay in wait for her in the office. She blew out the breath she'd sucked in. The pile of paperwork on her desk was larger than usual for some reason. That was when she said a silent prayer, hoping to conjure up a new case. The previous case they'd solved had left them all reeling. The suspect had been deluded and caused havoc in the community. She was still in the process of tying up the paperwork on that one. Fat chance of that happening with this lot to contend with. She stopped for a second to admire the view of the Brecon Beacons in the distance and then continued around the desk to her chair. She flopped into it.

Carla brought in a cup of coffee and placed it in the only clear spot on her desk. She let out a low whistle. "Planning on going home this evening, were you?"

Sara shrugged. "It's an impossible task trying to keep up with this sodding lot, day in, day out."

"Want me to share the load? It's not as if I have anything else to do, is it?"

"Thanks for the offer, but I'd better crack on with it myself. As you offered, what you can do for me, is have a look at the Mawdesley case. See if you can chase up the reports to finally put that one to bed."

"I can do that, no problem. Enjoy yourself." Carla grinned broadly and left the office.

Sara picked up the first brown envelope and tore the flap open. She placed it in the non-urgent pile and opened the next one. Half an hour later, her mind was numb. "Damn paperwork." How the fuck did the powers that be expect her to carry out her usual detective work when there was this mind-numbing shit to contend with on a daily basis?

Carla came to rescue her twenty minutes later. "How's it going, dare I ask?"

"Slowly." Sara sat back in her chair and studied her partner. "Why are your eyes sparkling?"

"We've got a code blue."

Sara sprang forward. "That doesn't explain the sparkle?"

"Sorry, my childish mind working overtime, imagining all sorts. The man was found naked in the river."

"Damn. Okay, I'll let you off. We should get over there. Where?"

"Down by the River Wye."

"Great. Don't tell me, he was found in a picturesque spot?"

"How did you guess? Dog walkers stumbled across him lying face-down, half on the bank and half in the water."

"Gosh, I bet that was a shock for them. Give me five minutes to tidy this lot away and I'll be with you. Scratch that, sod it, this can wait, a dead body can't."

They arrived at the scene to find the area cordoned off with tape. She was glad to see the SOCO team already there, struggling to erect a tent in the strong winds and rain.

"Is it worth the hassle?" Sara asked. "The body is wet anyway."

Lorraine, the pathologist, glared at her. "Yes, if only to preserve some dignity for the victim. You wouldn't believe I paid fifty quid to have my hair cut and styled last week, would you?"

"You were robbed," Sara said and laughed at the mortified expression on Lorraine's face.

"Well, that was rude and rather uncalled for, and you call yourself a bloody friend."

"Calm down, I was joking. Do you mind if we get on? I'm soaked through already."

"Some might say you deserve it after what you said about my hair."

Sara rolled her eyes and hugged her friend. "I was joshing with you. Have I touched a nerve? You're usually up for me ribbing you."

"Sorry. Feeling a tad emotional for some reason. Pulling my professional hat neatly into position. The victim is a blond gentleman, slim, tall, with an athletic build. I can't possibly tell you if he was handsome or not."

Sara prepared herself for the worst news possible. "Don't tell me someone has sliced off his face? Anything but that."

"Not exactly. His face and head are caved in. This attack was one of anger, hatred even. My guess is that the perp continued to pound the man's head and face with an object long after his death. I know what you're going to ask next: why? The truthful answer to that is, I don't know. But someone deliberately set out to obliterate the victim's features in a fierce, callous attack."

Sara swallowed down the bile burning her throat. "Okay, now you've prepared us for the worst, can we see him?"

Lorraine nodded and led the way through the slightly muddy area to the marquee that had now been fully erected on the bank of the river. Sara grinned and glanced down at Carla's pink boots. "Watch out for the muddy puddles there, partner. I'd hate for you to ruin those pretty boots of yours."

Carla growled and mumbled some kind of expletive that was indecipherable.

Sara couldn't help but chuckle as she followed Lorraine. Witnessing the victim's injuries for the first time, her grin soon disappeared. She ran a wet hand over her makeup-free face. "Jesus. I see what you mean."

Carla retched behind her and quickly left the tent.

"I'm surprised I didn't react the same way. That's horrendous. That poor man."

"It's tough. We've got used to such depravity over the years, haven't we?" Lorraine said.

"I have to say, back in Liverpool, I'd expect this type of thing. Not around here, though."

Lorraine pointed at her to gain her attention and then wagged her finger. "Now don't start all that bullshit about your being here has drawn out all the murderers in this county."

Sara stared at her, wide-eyed. "Why not? It's the truth, isn't it? The murder rate has escalated and shot through the damn roof since I moved to Hereford. Maybe I should jack it in and head back up north for the safety of the inhabitants of this area."

"That's bullshitting crap, and you know it. Put it down to a sign of the times. Half the murders committed today are copycat ones, injuries that perps have seen on a TV show and copied."

Sara nodded. "I suppose you're right, except, I haven't seen any shows lately where the perp has bashed someone's head to a pulp, have you?"

Lorraine shrugged. "You've got me there. All right, I admit, I was talking out of my backside, as normal."

Sara sniggered. "Okay, tell me what you know? Any ID found on him?"

"In case you haven't noticed, he's naked."

"Sorry, I didn't mean actually found on his person." Lorraine smiled. Sara swiped at her arm. "Stop winding me up. Didn't we pass a pile of clothes on the way to the scene?"

"We did. I'm glad your observation skills are up to scratch. I checked the man's clothes but found no ID, just a bunch of car keys."

Sara thought back to where she had parked the car, trying to remember if she'd seen a car other than those belonging to the professionals on site.

"I think there was a car outside the haulage firm at the entrance when we arrived. Do you want to see if the keys belong to that?" Lorraine asked.

"Worth a shot, right?"

"Stu, those car keys, get them and try them out on the car at the entrance, will you? Let us know the results."

The SOCO technician nodded and left the tent. Carla lifted the flap and joined them, her skin a subtle shade of green.

"Who found the body, do we know?" Sara asked, keeping her eyes on Lorraine instead of the victim.

"A couple of dog walkers. I think the first constable who arrived got down their details and sent them home rather than have them stand around in the pouring rain."

"Hard to believe people venture out in the rain with their dogs."

"Devoted animal lovers will do anything to keep their pets happy. My mum does the same with her poodle."

The tent flap was pulled back again, and Stu entered. "Yep, the keys opened the car, just like you thought they would."

Lorraine winked at Sara. "I'm clearly in the right job, eh?"

Sara laughed. "There's no denying that. Right, if you don't have anything else for us, we'll brave the elements again and set off to try and trace his next of kin. Crap, you don't fancy swapping jobs for the day, do you?"

"If you're up to doing a PM on the gent, then yes, I'm willing to give it a go."

"Er, scratch that. I'll call you later, after you've done the PM."

"You do that. Good luck."

Sara and Carla left the shelter of the tent and retraced their steps through the muddy field, past the pile of clothes which had been preserved with a plastic sheet covering them, and back to the vehicle.

Sara pressed the key fob and opened the car doors. Once inside, she rang the station. Jill Smalling answered.

"Jill, it's me. Do me a favour and run a plate for me." She read out the licence number of the black Audi sports car in front of her.

"I've got it. On it now. Want to remain on the line, boss?"

"Yep." She heard the sound of computer keys tapping and then silence until Jill spoke again.

"Here you go. The car is registered to a Lens Jensen of Jensen Haulage. His address is twenty-six Markham Drive, Tupsley."

"Thanks, Jill. We'll shoot over there and break the news to his family then come back to the station unless anything else crops up in the meantime. Can you and the rest of the team start the background checks on the victim? The usual, you know the drill."

"Will do, boss."

Sara ended the call, let out a large sigh and started the engine. "Let's get this over with. How are your boots?"

Carla glared at her. "Knackered. Okay, I admit you were right. Not the most practical colour to wear for work. I didn't know we'd get called out here, though, did I?"

"I'm always right. It's always best to plan for the unexpected, partner. That way we all save ourselves a lot of money, and no, you can't claim a new pair out of petty cash."

"The thought never even crossed my mind. I'll suffer the loss."

"They'll clean up a treat once the mud has dried up." Sara inched the vehicle past the SOCO van and a squad car and pulled onto the main road.

"Forgive me if I don't share your faith in that statement."

"Talking of which, make a note to chase up the witness statements when we get back to base. Maybe the dog walkers saw someone around the area at the time they were out."

"I bet they saw plenty of other dog walkers at that time of day, just saying."

"You're probably right. Why isn't a case ever cut and dried?"

"Because perps are getting smarter. Intent on putting us off the scent. If they made it easy for us, that wouldn't be as fulfilling for them. That's my take on it."

"You're probably right there. Whoever said it was easy being a copper must have a screw loose."

2

They arrived at the huge mansion around fifteen minutes later.

Waiting for the bell to be answered, Sara whispered, "Jensen. That's not English, or am I wrong?"

"Sounds Scandinavian to me. I seem to recall there being a John Jensen who played soccer a few years back."

Sara's eyebrows shot up. "Really? I had no idea you followed football."

"I don't. My dad used to force us to watch it. We weren't rich enough to own two TVs when I was a kid."

"Ah, I'm with you. Same with me, except Dad always insisted we watch black and white Westerns, starring John Wayne."

"Crikey, didn't realise you were that old."

Sara dug her in the ribs and tutted. "What's taking them so long to answer?"

"Maybe the rest of the family are away on holiday or out shopping. Want me to check around the back?"

Before Sara could answer, the door opened. A blonde woman, at least five feet eleven in her stocking feet stood there, looking them up and down as if they were a couple of tramps standing on her doorstep.

"Yes," she asked, although it sounded more like a command.

Sara and Carla both produced their IDs. "DI Sara Ramsey, and this is my partner, DS Carla Jameson. Are you Mrs Jensen?"

"Yes. Why? What brings the police to my door?"

Sara detected a slight accent to her tone. "Would you mind if we come in for a chat, Mrs Jensen?"

"Not unless you tell me what this is all about. They could be fake IDs for all I know."

"Feel free to check by ringing Hereford police station, it's your prerogative."

"I think I will. You haven't told me what this visit is about?" She withdrew her mobile from the back pocket of her slim-fit leopardskin trousers and messed around with the screen. Her attention lost for a while, Sara decided to keep quiet. Finally finding the number she was searching for, Mrs Jensen dialled it and spoke to someone. She looked sheepish when she ended the call.

"Sorry, you can't be too careful these days. Come in."

"We don't blame you in the slightest," Sara replied, stepping past the large oak front door into an expansive white hallway with its grand, sweeping metal staircase. She couldn't help but think she'd stepped into the pages of a top magazine.

The woman seemed bored with Sara's awe. "Are you going to tell me what this is all about?"

Keen to see more of the woman's beautiful home, Sara said, "Can we go somewhere more comfortable?"

"I can see you won't be satisfied until you see more of the house. Come through to the kitchen. Do you want a drink?"

"Thanks, two coffees would be wonderful."

The woman flounced on the spot and headed towards the rear of the house. A massive glass wall ran along the length of the room, which led on to a large grey stone patio area with an enormous jacuzzi tub sitting on one end and fancy outdoor furniture on the other. The furniture was bordered by a raised area full of brightly coloured plants. Sara wondered if the plants were fake—they appeared far too perfect to be real.

The woman led them over to a state-of-the-art kitchen with a combination of stainless steel and white gloss surfaces which took Sara's breath away. She predicted the kitchen alone would have set the woman and her fella back around a hundred grand.

"Instant or freshly brewed?" Mrs Jensen asked.

"Instant will do fine. We don't want to put you to any bother."

"No bother. I only ever have freshly brewed. I know it's an acquired taste, though, that's why I gave you the option."

"In that case, we'll join you."

Mrs Jensen nodded and motioned for them to sit on the stainless steel stools on the other side of the kitchen island, the surface of which was made of a brushed steel.

Sara and Carla both hopped up on the stools. Together, they watched the woman expertly fill the container with water, insert it in the fancy machine and place the coffee powder into the receptacle that she then attached to the machine. Within seconds, the water had heated up and coffee filtered through into a glass jug beneath. The smell was exceptional and made Sara reflect on her childhood, when she used to walk through the high street, past Carwardine's, envious of the patrons inside, sampling the delicious-smelling coffee. She supposed they were the original baristas, so much better than all the Costas popping up today, in her opinion.

"There you go, ladies. Now, perhaps you'll tell me what this visit is about?"

Sara placed her hand around the tiny cup filled with strong coffee. She didn't have the heart to ask for any milk which she presumed would considerably alter the flavour. "Thank you, you're very kind. Can I ask where your husband is?"

"At work, at the haulage firm," Mrs Jensen said, a tiny frown appearing on her tanned forehead.

"When was the last time you spoke to him?"

"Yesterday, around eight. He told me he was going to work late and would crash at work. He often does that during the month. Our business is ultra-busy at this time of the year."

"I see. And you haven't bothered to ring him this morning?"

"We're not a loved-up young couple, Inspector. My husband and I know the value of giving each other space in a marriage."

"I understand."

"Do you?" she bit back quickly. "What's this all about? Why are you asking me these questions?"

Sara took a sip from her hot drink and burnt the roof of her mouth. *Shit, why didn't I wait?* "Forgive me, I'm simply trying to get some background." She paused, inhaled a large breath, and then continued, "I'm sorry to have to inform you that your husband's body was discovered this morning."

Mrs Jensen's frown deepened, and her head shook, slowly at first and then vigorously as the news sank in. "No. Not Lens. His body? Are you telling me he's dead?"

Sara nodded. "I'm sorry. Yes, his body was pulled out of the river, close to his haulage firm."

"The river? I don't understand. What was he doing by the river? He hated the water. Oh God, did he fall in and drown? Oh my, why? Why would he take the risk?"

"What risk?" Sara asked, jumping on something she'd highlighted as a possible clue.

"The risk of going near the water when he hated it. Why? What did you think I meant?" Tears were slow in forming, but when they came, they ran down her cheeks faster than an avalanche of snow gathering momentum down the Eiger.

"Sorry, I misunderstood." Sara sighed heavily. "The thing is, Mrs Jensen…"

"It's Mie, pronounced Me-A."

"Thank you. The thing is, Mie, I'm sorry to have to tell you that your husband was murdered."

She sat back on her stool. Luckily, there were upright stainless steel bars to support her. "Did he drown? How do you know he was murdered?"

"No, he didn't drown. I suspect he was dead long before he hit the water. I don't really want to go into detail. I don't think that would be very fair. It would be better for you to remember him the way he was."

Sara glanced around for a possible photograph of the couple, but the room was bare of any knick-knacks.

"I can't believe this." Mie buried her head in her hands and sobbed. "Why?" She asked, emotion straining her voice.

"We've yet to establish that. Maybe you can help us?"

Her hands dropped from her mascara-stained face. "Me? What would I know?"

"You can possibly tell us if your husband has had any problems lately. Maybe with one of his drivers. Has he sacked anyone? Perhaps someone had a grudge against him and sought out their revenge."

"No, nothing that I can think of. Please, my head is all over the place. I can't think, not now. I need to take it all in, not be bombarded with questions that I just don't have the answer to."

"I'm sorry, I didn't mean to be so insensitive. It's just that if we can ask the questions early on, there's a possibility we'll trace the murderer quicker than if we leave it a few days. I'm sure you can understand that."

"I get that. But you have to understand that my head is spinning right now. His family are back in Denmark; they'll be devastated when they learn of his death. We've been living in this country since our teens, never dreamt anything along these lines would happen. How the heck am I going to break the news to his elderly and infirm mother? This could finish her off. Bloody hell." She covered her face once more and sobbed, long and hard.

Sara's own eyes filled with tears, and she glanced Carla's way to see the emotion written on her face as well. *God, I hate this job sometimes. The grief we have to witness at the loss of a loved one. There has to be more to life than this!* She remained silent, letting Mie grieve for a moment or two, thinking it would be heartless for her to press the woman.

Eventually, Mie's hands dropped again, and she withdrew a lace hanky from a drawer beside her. "I'm sorry for breaking down. I'm usually such a strong person, but this has hit me harder than I anticipated."

"Please, you have nothing to apologise for. Everyone deals with their grief differently. Are you up to answering more questions now or would you rather leave it for today?"

"I want to get it out of the way; however, I think I should notify the family as soon as I can."

"I get that. We'll leave you for today and call back in a day or two, if that's all right with you?" Sara realised it contradicted what she'd said earlier but she was always cautious where a spouse's grief was concerned.

"I think I'll be ready to answer your questions by then. Thank you for your kindness and understanding."

"Maybe you can put together a list of your husband's friends and work colleagues. Sorry if you think that's too much to ask. It'll make our lives easier if we get that kind of information sooner rather than later."

"Once I've contacted my family, I'll sit down and do that for you."

Mie walked them back through the house and bid them farewell at the door. Sara handed her a business card and told her to contact her when she was ready to speak to them.

On the walk back to the car, Carla breathed out a heavy sigh. "That was tough. She was devastated."

"Understatement of the century that, partner. Doesn't help us much. We'll have to see if the team have found out anything yet."

"We could take it upon ourselves to go to the haulage firm and start asking questions."

"I hate to do that behind the wife's back...however, we haven't got much else to go on at present. Okay, yes, let's do that."

When they arrived back near the crime scene, instead of parking in their previous spot, they drove through the large metal gates and drew up outside the main office of the haulage business. A lady with long brunette hair, grey patches on either side above her ears, looked up and smiled as they entered.

"Good morning, ladies. What can I do for you?"

Sara showed her ID. "DI Sara Ramsey. Is it possible to speak with the person in charge?"

"Damn, is this to do with what's happened outside?"

"Possibly. Who's in charge around here?"

"That would be Mr Jensen. He appears to be very late today."

"Is there a second in charge perhaps?"

"Mr Lockwood, Andy. He's here. Shall I ask if he has time to speak to you?"

"Ask him to make time, it's important."

"I'll ring him now. Excuse me a moment."

Sara and Carla stepped away from the desk, allowing her some privacy.

The receptionist placed the call then rose from her chair. "If you'd like to follow me, ladies."

Sara smiled and nodded. They left the reception area and walked up a short corridor to an office where a man in his early forties was waiting for them in front of a large oak desk. He held out his hand. "Andy Lockwood. Please take a seat. Thank you, Maureen."

The receptionist exited the room and closed the door behind her. Mr Lockwood took his seat, a puzzled expression set in place. "Sorry, I didn't catch your names?"

"DI Sara Ramsey, and this is my partner, DS Carla Jameson."

"Thank you. Okay, now the formalities are out of the way, what can I do for you?"

"How much do you know about what's been going on down by the river today?" Sara asked.

The man leaned forward in his chair and linked his hands on the desk. "Not much. I overheard a couple of dog walkers as they passed by. They were discussing a possible murder. I wasn't sure if they were talking about a programme they'd seen on the TV or something."

"You heard correct. There was a murder overnight. The victim, I'm sorry to have to tell you, is Lens Jensen."

Lockwood's face instantly drained of all colour, and he flopped back in his chair, clearly dumbstruck by the news.

"Are you all right, sir?" Sara asked, concerned.

"Stunned beyond words. Are you sure it's him?" He ran a hand over his face and shook his head slowly.

"Yes, we've just come from his house where we had to break the news to his wife."

"Heck, poor Mie. I bet she was distraught by the news."

"As to be expected, if they were a close couple. Didn't you notice his car outside when you came into work this morning?"

"No. I can't say I did. I don't tend to function normally until the third coffee hits my brain. I can't believe this. Damn, was he murdered then?"

"Yes, we believe so. Maybe you can help us with our enquiries."

"Of course, I'll do what I can to help. You'll have to forgive me if I screw up a little. This news has shocked the hell out of me."

"We'll make allowances. Maybe you can start off by telling us what type of man Mr Jensen was?"

"As a businessman he was ruthless, wiped the floor with his competitors in order to get a lucrative contract."

"How many years has the business been running?"

"Twenty plus, I've forgotten exactly."

"That's a long time. You say he 'wiped the floor with his competitors'. Are you saying that he could have possibly made a few enemies along the way?"

His head tilted from side to side. "Like any business, it's possible, not that I've ever seen any proof of that. That's not to say he hasn't had the occasional bust-up with a competitor over the years but, as far as I know, he's always made it up with them. Damn! You don't think one of them could've bumped him off, do you?"

"We have to keep an open mind on that for now. Have there been any major deals in the air lately, one that could have caused a competitor some grief?"

"Not recently. Maybe six months ago, but nothing in the last few months. To be honest with you, we're stretched to the limits at present. We'd be hard pressed to take on another contract."

"Would you mind giving us a list of your competitors, anyone likely to have a grudge against your boss?"

"I can come up with a short list of names, but I wouldn't say any of them could be classed as murderers. What am I saying? Watching the news every night, and they show murderers on the screen. None of them seem the type to take someone's life. God, am I prattling on or what? Sorry, put it down to the shock."

Sara smiled. "Try and sort out a list for us. We'll do some digging and see what we can come up with."

He pulled a spiral bound pad from the drawer in his desk and jotted down several names and addresses then tore off the sheet of paper and handed it across the desk to Sara.

"That's brilliant, thanks very much. What about the staff? By that I mean, have you had any problems with the drivers recently, you know, possibly having to sack someone for breaking the company's rules, anything along those lines?"

"No, nothing at all. All our drivers are loyal and value their jobs. Been with us from the year dot some of them."

"That's quite unusual, isn't it?"

"Definitely is. Lens has always treated his drivers well, paid them over the going rate to get the best out of them. I can't see anyone wanting to kill him." He shuddered a little. "God, it's just sinking in now that I'll never share another rude joke with him over a pint down the pub. He had a wicked sense of humour."

"It can take a while for grief to set in. Maybe you can tell me what his family life was like? Did he have any children?"

"Yes, Lizzie, she's eighteen and away at university."

"Where?"

"Up in Newcastle. She comes home when she can, every few months or so."

"What is she studying?"

"Psychology. She's hoping to be a shrink at the end of the course."

"I see. And his wife, Mie, did they get on well?"

His gaze drifted down to the desk, and he chewed on his bottom lip for a moment or two.

"Did they?" Sara prompted.

"Yes and no. They had their ups and downs. I think more downs than ups lately, in truth."

Sara glanced out of the corner of her eye to see Carla taking notes. "Do you know what the problems were about by any chance?"

"Him putting it around mostly. Poking his dick where he shouldn't have been poking it."

"He had affairs? How many and how frequently?"

"Yep. Not sure how Mie put up with it for so long. He told me they had one of those open marriages. I never heard him mention that she ever had another man on the go, though."

"So a one-sided open marriage then?"

He shrugged. "If there is such a thing. Shame really. Mie is a real beauty, in spite of her age." He winced. "Ouch, did I really say that out loud? Sorry. I guess I still feel twenty-five myself, even if my years are advancing quickly."

Sara chuckled. "I think we all think of ourselves as being younger when the grey hairs appear. I don't suppose he discussed the ins and outs of his relationships with these women, did he?"

"Sometimes. I kind of switched off when he went into detail. Maybe it was slight jealousy on my part. To know he had a beautiful wife waiting for him at home and him dipping his wick elsewhere, it didn't sit well with me, shall we say."

"How many affairs are we talking about?"

"Gosh, how long is a piece of string?"

Sara cringed. "And Mie knew about every affair?"

He blew out his cheeks and sat forward. "Not sure if she knew about every one of them. I tried to get him to tame his wandering eye, but it was like talking to that damn wall behind you sometimes."

"He was stubborn then?"

"Extremely."

"Did you ever fall out with him?"

"Occasionally, for a few hours, no more than that. Don't think I had anything to do with his death."

"It's fine, I think you're in the clear. Where did he meet these women?"

"Mainly at the pubs and eateries in town. They were all local. Told me he preferred to have his sex on tap and living around the corner. Crude concept, eh?"

"Very crude indeed. I don't suppose you can give us any names of the women he was involved with?"

"I was past caring after a while. Fed up with him bragging about his latest conquests. He got the hint and clammed up about it, eventually."

"Any names at all?"

"Why? You think maybe one of them could've killed him now? No...he didn't have his dick cut off, did he?" His eyes widened at the thought.

"No. Not as far as we know. We could really do with finding these women. Perhaps some of them were married or had a boyfriend..."

He clicked his fingers and pointed at her. "And you think one of their other halves might have done this. Well, that would make more sense than a woman killing him, I suppose."

His amateur detective skills were beginning to tick Sara off. "It's not definite, sir, although it could likely go that way once the investigation begins in earnest. Hence why we need more names to go on."

"I can't help you. All I can tell you is that he picked women who were single. Who knows these days if they were telling him the truth or not? Maybe they just told him that once he started flashing his cash around."

"It's a shame you can't supply us with any names to proceed with. Do you think the bar staff at any of the establishments in town would be able to help us?"

He shrugged again. "You can try; you'll have to ask them. I'm sorry I can't be any more help."

"I'll leave you a card in case anything comes to mind in the next few days, once things have settled down a little." Sara slid a card across the desk and rose from her chair.

Carla tucked her notebook in her pocket and did the same.

He saw them back to the reception area and shook their hands. Sara was contemplative on the journey to the car.

Once inside, Carla asked, "Does all this add up to you?"

Sara sighed. "Not right now, no. Funny that Mie didn't tell us about his infidelity. Saying that, she didn't really tell us much because of the shock. I don't want to cast aspersions or speak ill of the dead, but could this be a Danish thing? I seem to remember something I read in a magazine once about them being sex mad. I could be wrong. Worth looking into; however, that information alone won't help us to solve the case."

"You're more knowledgeable about the Danish than me. I know nothing about them."

"What good it's going to do us, I don't know. Damn, we're no further forward, are we?"

Carla waved a sheet of paper in Sara's face. "Wrong. We have the competitors' names that need delving into."

"True. Let's get back to base and crack on with that."

3

The afternoon dragged by. The team had their heads down and were busy dealing with all the background checks into the deceased, and Sara left Carla chasing up the competitors, but everything drew a blank. If anything, the owners of the other haulage firms in the area all sounded genuinely stunned when her partner had spoken to them. The team found out that Lens Jensen and his wife had moved to the UK over twenty years earlier. He set up his haulage firm within a few months. A search of Companies House records showed that the business had increased in value every year in the past ten years and was now worth over ten million pounds. Sara assumed that fortune would now be going to his wife, Mie.

The team didn't find much in his background relating to his family back in Denmark, only that his father used to be a pilot for their regional airline. His mother died when he was a child at the age of five. Maybe his father had different women coming through the house every week, and that was where he'd picked up his Lothario ways. That scenario might be way off the mark, though, and one that Sara had thought up as a possibility in light of what she'd learnt from Andy Lockwood. The truth was, until the post-mortem report came in, they were in trouble.

Frustrated, she picked up the phone. "Lorraine, I'm hoping you've had a chance to open up the victim found this morning."

"Good afternoon to you, too. You'd be wrong about that. Another case was waiting for me when I got back. I'm understaffed, as you are. It's a case of first come, first served, and the copper dealing with the case wanted to be involved with the PM, unlike *some* people I could mention."

"Bugger off. I know a dig when I hear one. I don't have to attend them. There's nothing in my contract that states I have to watch you slice open another human being and stick your hand inside to extract their organs."

"You make it sound as if I get off on it."

"Deep down, I think you do. You have to have a warped mind to want to become a pathologist in the first place, right?"

Lorraine laughed. "Get you. I suppose you have a point on that one, I'll give you that. Anyway, if you want me to get to your victim, I can't stand around chatting to you, especially as I have a hot date this evening."

"Oh, tell me more?"

"Not a cat in hell's chance, lady. That's my secret to keep for the interim. Ha! That's got your little brain working overtime, hasn't it?"

"Nope," Sara snapped, lying. "Get back to me ASAP with the results. There was a time when you'd hang around at work with the stiffs until you cleared the backlog."

"Ooo...hark at you. Bitchy comments like that aren't going to force the name out of me."

"Whatever. Have fun on your secret date. I'm sure you'll be gloating soon enough if everything works out well for you this evening."

"You're right there. I'll share all the details when the deed is done."

"Ew...spare me that, if you will. Speak soon."

Lorraine was laughing when she ended the call.

Sara felt drained, the same as she always did at the beginning of a case when all they did was go round and round in a never-ending circle, chasing their damn tails. She left her office at five to six and clapped to gain the team's attention. "Right, go home, everyone. Thanks for all your efforts today. Tomorrow is another day, as they say. Have a good evening."

The team all seemed relieved to be going home. Carla and Sara collected their jackets and left the incident room, switching off the lights as they went.

"Are you all right?" Sara asked her subdued partner.

"Yes and no, if you must know."

"What's wrong? Work or personal?"

Carla shook her head. "I wish I frigging knew. I have a feeling something horrendous is going to happen in the imminent future. You ever get a feeling like that?"

"Sometimes. Not often, though. Want to talk about it over a drink? I'm free until about eight."

"Would you mind if I took a rain check?"

"No, not at all. Can I just say that I'm a little concerned about you right now, is that allowed?"

"Honestly, there's no need for you to worry—at least I hope there's not. Let's hope the feeling I have subsides overnight. As you rightly told the team earlier, tomorrow is another day."

By this time, they had descended the stairs and exited the main entrance to the station.

"Okay, but promise me that if you need me, you'll ring me. Even if it's at three in the morning."

"I doubt it'll come to that, but thanks, that means a lot. What plans have you got tonight?"

"Nothing much. Mark won't be home for a few hours. He has an op to perform. I might drop by and see how Dad is. Yep, if I can't persuade you to go for a drink, then I'll go and see how my folks are both doing."

"Great news. Sending them my love, not that they know me from Adam. What the heck am I on about?"

Sara laughed. "Fucked if I know, matey. But the thought was there. Enjoy your evening. Sink a few glasses of wine to drive that feeling of uncertainty away."

"I might do that. I'll see how the evening pans out. Gary is working, so no chance of seeing him tonight."

"That's a shame. I'm sensing you could do with a cuddle from your man. I'd offer you one but I doubt it will have the same effect."

"I'm not that desperate," Carla replied and hastily retreated to her car.

Sara smiled and slipped into her own vehicle. She turned the radio on to try to catch the six o'clock news and caught the tail end of what the reporter had to say about the case they were investigating. As usual at this stage in the enquiry, the reporter's account of the facts was sketchy at best. She knew she'd have to call a press conference soon to appease the media, but with very little to go on, that might prove pointless at this stage. She'd think about that overnight.

She drove the fifteen- to twenty-minute journey to her parents' house in Marden—she rang ahead much to her mother's relief and disappointment. Relief that she was making a visit. Disappointment that she'd turned down the chance to have dinner with them.

The road was quiet when she got out of the car. She lived in the next village, in a similar idyllic rural location. She breathed in the fresh air and approached her parents' front door. Her father opened it before she had a chance to insert her key.

"Hello, love. Come in, it's wonderful to see you."

She smiled and kissed him on the cheek as she entered the house. "How's the invalid doing?"

"Cheeky! I'm doing okay." He leaned in close and whispered, "I think I'd be doing better if your mother didn't insist on fussing over me twenty-four hours a day."

Sara tutted. "Admit it, you're enjoying all the attention."

He winked and smiled then held his finger and thumb an inch apart. "Between you and me, maybe just a teeny bit."

"You'd soon complain if she ignored you, old man."

He roared with laughter. "Now ain't that the truth. Come on, she's in the kitchen, baking."

"At this time of night? You've had your dinner, haven't you?"

"Yes, we've not long finished that. Now don't stop her, she's knocking up a few scones for you to take back home with you. Shame you couldn't join us for dinner, Sara."

"I know. I had to consider Mark, though, Dad. He'll be expecting a meal when he gets home later."

"I know. Maybe you two can join us over the weekend for a barbeque if the weather is nice."

"We'll see. The forecast isn't great for the rest of the week."

They walked through the house and into the kitchen where her mother was busy rolling out the scone mixture on a floured board on the kitchen table. "Hi, Mum, how's it diddling?"

"You are funny with your little sayings. Things are going well, now that your father has finally realised I know what I'm talking about."

"That's so unfair," her father protested from the doorway.

"Stop complaining and put the kettle on. I'm sure our daughter won't say no to a coffee after a long day at work."

"I'd love one, thanks. I've missed you two bickering and tiptoeing around each other lately. It tells me that life is slowly returning to normal for you both."

"Not sure if that's a good thing or bad," her father muttered.

Her mother finished using the cutter on the scone mixture and picked up a little excess and threw it at her father, which hit him on the side of the face.

"Oi, there's no need to start a food fight."

They all laughed and spent the next thirty minutes talking about her father's health and the exercise regime the hospital had insisted putting him on since his near death and subsequent bypass operation.

It was good to see her parents looking less anxious and with smiles on their faces. Sara was in the process of saying goodbye when her sister walked through the front door.

Lesley had been due to get married last week, but it had been decided by everyone to postpone the wedding for a few months.

"Hi, Lesley, you seem harassed. Is everything okay?" Sara asked.

Lesley's cheeks coloured up. "You're such an amazing detective. No, everything is far from okay, if you must know."

Sara got the feeling she was about to regret asking that particular question, given the time of night and her imminent departure. Her sister was a bit of a drama queen and was prone to blowing things up out of all proportion. She erred on the side of caution and asked, "Can we help at all?"

"Yes, I suppose you can, being a copper."

Sara frowned. "Meaning what? Do you want to get to the point, sis? I was just about to leave. Mark will be expecting me."

"Go then, see if I care," Lesley bit back.

Sara rubbed at her eyes and heaved out a sigh. "Can you stop sniping at me and tell me what this is all about?"

Lesley flopped into a kitchen chair, their parents standing close to her, worried expressions on their faces. Sara hated what her sister's histrionics were doing to their anxiety levels. She felt like slapping her sister around the face and telling her to grow up even though she had no idea what the problem was.

"Okay, you have our attention. Tell us what's wrong?" She wanted to add, *and make it quick*, but thought better of it.

"The wedding is off."

"What? Why?" Sara asked, beating her parents to the two most important questions.

"Brendan has repeatedly lied to me. He's sitting at home now, sporting a black eye and several other injuries."

"You assaulted him?"

Her sister glared at her. "What do you take me for? No, a loan shark has beaten him up."

"Oh my," their mother said.

"Mum, Dad, why don't you sit down? Better still, why don't you both go in the lounge and let me get the facts from Lesley?"

"Not on your nelly," her father replied obstinately, dragging out a chair and sitting next to Lesley.

Her mother did the same but sat between Sara and her sister.

"Okay, now you've got everyone's attention, why don't you start from the beginning and we'll see what we can come up with to help get you out of this situation?"

Her sister snorted. "Unless you've got seventy grand lying around,

I doubt there's anything anyone can do to help. Anyway, I've told him to pack his bags and get out."

"Wow, seventy grand, is that how much he owes the loan shark?" Sara demanded.

"I just said so, didn't I?"

Sara cringed at her sister's venomous tone; however, she was willing to forgive her in the circumstances and let it pass. "How long has this loan been in place?"

"The past two years. I didn't have a damn clue. He's been gambling, betting on horses and playing damn poker behind my back. Can you believe that? Because I bloody well can't. Who would do such a thing, and how has he managed to keep it a secret from me all this time? I wish I'd never laid eyes on the man. No wonder he was always asking after Dad's health. He probably had an eye on any inheritance due to me. Sorry, Dad, I didn't mean to share that with you, it just came out."

Their father placed a hand over Lesley's. "It's all right, love. I guess we never really know what's going on with the people we love until something like this rears its head, isn't that right, Sara?"

"If you say so, Dad. I'm shocked to hear this, Lesley. Are you sure there's not some way around this?" Sara asked.

Lesley stared at her and shook her head slowly. "Not for me, no. Once the trust has gone in a relationship, there's no way of gaining that trust back."

"If you're unwilling to make your relationship work, then there's very little we can say to try and change your mind. I'm sorry this has happened to you."

"That's not all. I think this loan shark is going to come after me next." Lesley burst into tears.

Sara placed an arm around her shoulder and gently asked, "What makes you think that, Lesley?"

"He told me."

"Who? The loan shark?"

"No, silly, Brendan did. Last week I was going through my paperwork and noticed something strange. A letter had arrived that I didn't open—it was shoved in my file. It was from the mortgage company, stating they had altered my deeds to reflect my request to add Brendan to them. I had requested no such thing."

"No! Are you saying that Brendan forged your signature?" Sara's heart pounded harder.

"So it would appear. When I told him to leave the house, he said he wouldn't as he jointly owned it. Everything slotted into place then. I say again, how the heck can I trust someone as deceitful as him? Not only that, but he's told the loan shark that we're going to sell the house to pay off his debts, and there's not a damn thing I can do about it."

"Oh, dear God, that's simply terrible, Lesley," their mother said, near to tears herself.

"Okay, first of all, we can get Brendan on a fraud charge and get that document reversed. It'll cost you a packet in solicitor's fees, I'm guessing."

"Money I don't have," Lesley whined.

"Nonsense, we'll help cover the costs," their mother said.

"I'd offer to chip in, but money is tight since buying my own house," Sara added, genuinely sorry.

"Thank you. I'm so grateful, Mum and Dad. I haven't slept for days. How did it come to this? I feel duped. He's taken me for a fool. No, worse than that. Ugh, I don't think I'll ever trust another human being again, except for you guys, as long as I live."

"Where is he now, Lesley?" Sara asked, rubbing her sister's hand, trying to comfort her.

"At home. He's refusing to leave. Oh shit, what if he locks me out, refuses to let me back in the house? I never thought of that." She openly sobbed, pulling at Sara's heartstrings.

"It's okay, we'll find a way round this, Lesley. The law is on your side, we just need to prove it. Maybe you can stay here with Mum and Dad for a while."

"Of course you can. Sara's right, he's in the wrong, Lesley. We'll help you prove that he is, too."

"What would I do without you? I'm so sorry to bring this to your door after what's happened to Dad."

"Nonsense, I'm as fit as a fiddle and getting stronger every day," their father stated proudly.

"But what if the worry of all this mess sets you back? I'll never be able to forgive myself if that happens."

"It won't come to that," Sara assured her. "Will it, Dad? You're going to promise me not to get het up, aren't you?"

"I promise to remain calm. It's a good job we've got a copper in the family, that's all I can say. Now, are you going to stay here with us or brave it out at home with that bugger?"

"What do you think I should do, honestly?" Lesley asked Sara.

"I would remain at the house, even if you live in separate rooms to him. At least you'll be there to prevent him from selling off the furniture and things like that."

"He wouldn't?" Lesley appeared shocked by the notion. "What about when I'm out at work, though?"

"I wouldn't put it past the scoundrel if he's forged your signature on a legal document. There's no telling what lengths he'll go to. The key is to keep schtum. If he asks you anything about your intentions, don't tell him. Keep him guessing. You need to jot everything down in a notebook. Do you know the name of this loan shark?"

"Mick somebody. I suppose I can get it for you. Do you think he'll come and strip the house?"

"Not if we can put things into action immediately. Oh dear, you have got yourself in a pickle. I have to say, he's always appeared a little shifty to me."

"Why on earth didn't you say something?"

Sara raised an eyebrow and asked, "If I'd said anything disparaging about him, you would have torn me in two. Go on, admit it, sis?"

"I'd do no such thing. Well, maybe a few weeks ago, but not now. He deserves everything coming his way. I hate him."

"Now, Lesley, you mustn't say that," their mother reprimanded.

"Why not? It's the truth. To think I've had that man in my bed… sorry, I'll stop there," Lesley began, halting when she saw the look of shock on their parents' faces.

"Do you want me to come home with you, in case there's any trouble?" Sara asked.

"Would you? That would put my mind at ease if you did."

"Want to go now?"

"I can see you're eager to get home. Okay, let's go back now. I'm so sorry to dump all this worry on you, Mum and Dad."

"Nonsense, your sister will guide you through this mess and out the other side, love. You two get off," their father said.

"I'll make the scones. Maybe you can drop in tomorrow and pick them up on your way home from work, Sara?"

"I'll see, Mum. We started a new investigation today. Haven't got a clue how that's going to proceed over the next few days."

"Sorry for adding to your burden," Lesley replied, sighing and drying her tears on a tissue she'd pulled from the box on the kitchen table.

"Hush now, you're doing no such thing. Come on."

Sara and Lesley left the house. Their parents waved them off at the front door. Sara followed her sister's car through the winding narrow lanes to her semi-detached house fifteen minutes away. Every conceivable light was on from what Sara could tell.

"Blimey, has he done that on purpose, or do you always light up the neighbourhood at this time of night?"

"It's a regular occurrence with him. I'll be glad when he moves out permanently. It's cost a bundle in utility bills running this place. His disrespect for money should have been a warning sign for me when we first started dating. Never dreamt it would come to this."

"Love is blind, sis. We'll sort it, don't you fret. I'm sorry you have to go back in there, but it's for your own peace of mind. There's no telling what damage he or anyone else could do to the property if you moved out. I'm going to put in a call when I get home, ask a patrol car to keep a regular eye on the place if they're in the area."

"Thank you, you're one in a million. I really didn't want to lay this on your shoulders. You have enough to do, without worrying about what's happening to me."

"Nonsense. At the end of the day, you're family, and that's what families do, they stick together and work out possible solutions which will make life easier for everyone. Come on, I want to see what his reaction is when you show up with me in tow."

"God, I hope he doesn't kick off. I'm not as strong as you, Sara, I never have been."

She rubbed her sister's arm and smiled. "That'll change over the coming months. It has to, sis, if we're going to combat him."

"I wish I had your faith. Deep breath. I think I'm ready."

Lesley inserted the key in the front door and opened it. Sara nodded for her to continue, and together they entered the property. They'd only gone a few feet when Brendan emerged on the landing above and shouted down at them.

"What's she doing here? I might have known you'd call in the reinforcements."

Sara pulled her sister's arm and stepped in front of her. "What do you think you're playing at? Why rack up all those debts and keep Lesley in the dark the way you have? What the hell did that achieve? Look at the state of you. I'm telling you now, lay one hand on Lesley, and it'll be the last thing you do on this earth, and yes, take that as a threat, Brendan."

He threw his arms out to the sides and let them go so they slapped helplessly against his thighs. "I didn't mean for any of this to happen. I admit, it was foolish of me to get into so much debt. I feel stupid. Babe, we can work this out between us. Seek advice from a debt counsellor if you're willing to stand beside me."

"Why should she? It's too late for that. For Christ's sake, you were planning a wedding. You know the costs involved in that. Why the heck didn't you tell Lesley about the trouble you were in? Why let it get this far?"

"I don't know. I thought I could handle it myself. Now that she knows, we can tackle it together and get out of this mess as a team."

"A *team*? Are you serious? You seem to be forgetting there's no I in team, and all this appears to be about is the mess you've got yourself into."

"I know I was wrong…Lesley, say something."

"I can't speak to you. I want you out of here and out of my life," Lesley replied, her voice quivering with pain.

Brendan shrugged. "It ain't gonna happen. This house is as much mine now as it is yours."

"We'll see about that," Sara replied. "A word of warning for you, Brendan: you touch my sister, and I promise you I'll get you banged up on numerous charges, made up charges if I have to."

"Is that a threat, Inspector Ramsey?"

"No, it's a *promise*. Get your act together and leave this house. You've got two weeks in which to find alternative accommodation. You hear me?"

He issued her a challenging glare. "Then what? Because I assure you, I'm staying put."

"You'll find out. I'd hate to reveal what I have planned for you at this early stage. Be mindful that I have influential people I can call out, some on the right side of the law and others who aren't. Don't force me to get the latter characters involved—you're going to wish you hadn't."

"Your threats won't work on me. My name is on the deeds now, and there isn't a damn thing you or anyone else can do about it."

"We'll see. I've told Lesley to ring me day or night if you cause a problem."

He left the landing and went into one of the bedrooms.

Sara turned to face her sister and pulled her into her arms. She whispered in her ear, "Stay strong, hon. We won't let the bastard win. I'll have a chat with a solicitor friend of mine; she'll advise us how to proceed. Ring me if you need me."

"Thanks so much, Sara. I'll make something to eat, not that I'm hungry, and stock up with drinks and lock myself in my bedroom when you've gone."

"Make sure you have your mobile with you as well."

"I will. Sorry I got you involved in this, I never meant to."

"Don't be." Sara hugged Lesley, pecked her on the cheek and left.

She glanced up at the window of the bedroom at the front to find Brendan glaring at her. She remained there for a few moments, holding his stare, refusing to be intimidated by him. He gave in first and walked away from the window. Sara settled herself in the car and started the engine.

She hated leaving her sister in such a hostile environment. That was the trouble when you knew the law inside out, and there wasn't a damn thing you could do about a predicament as volatile as that in which her sister had found herself in.

She drove home, her mind full of different scenarios, some good and some exceptionally bad. Mark's car was outside the house when she got home. She parked, locked up her vehicle for the night and walked up the path.

"Everything all right, Sara? You looked miles away then."

The voice behind startled her. "Sorry, Ted, I didn't see you there. Tough day at work. Still going over things in my mind."

"You don't have to apologise. You need a nice chilled glass of wine down your neck and to put your feet up this evening. I hope that young man of yours has started on your dinner. If he hasn't, give us a knock, and I'm sure Mavis will have something suitable in the freezer you can defrost. You work too hard, lass."

"I know. Thanks for the offer. I think I can smell something cooking. Have a good evening. If the weather is good on Saturday, why don't you both join us for dinner?"

"Let's not make plans yet and jinx the damn weather. Your invite is duly noted, thank you. Enjoy your evening, what's left of it."

"I will. Speak soon."

She waved at her neighbour and opened the front door to find Mark in the kitchen knocking up something in the wok.

"Hey you. I was worried when you weren't here."

"Long day and an even longer evening. I'll tell you all about it after dinner. What are you cooking?"

"Chicken stir-fry. Thought I'd tackle something healthy for a change." He reached into the cupboard next to him and withdrew a couple of glasses. "Pour us a wine each, it's in the fridge. I stopped by the off-licence on the way home."

"You're amazing. With pleasure, I could sure do with one. How did the operation go?"

"It turned out to be easier than anticipated, hence me being home at my usual time. You look knackered."

"I am. Mentally tired. Can I make a call? I won't be two seconds and then I'll tell you about the drama that was waiting for me at Mum and Dad's."

He swiftly turned to face her. "Has your dad had a relapse? Is it his heart again?"

"No, nothing like that. Bear with me."

He frowned and nodded then got back to tossing the vegetables in the pan.

Sara took her mobile into the lounge and flopped onto the sofa. *Bugger, I shouldn't have done that. I fear I'm not going to be able to get up again now.* She rang her friend and confidante, Cynthia Wallis.

"Hello, Sara. To what do I owe the pleasure at this time of night?"

"Sorry to call so late. I need a little personal advice concerning a member of my family."

"Sounds serious. I'm cooking dinner at the moment. If I can put you on speaker and you don't mind the sound of pots and pans clanging in your ear, I can do two things at once."

"Fantastic. Not sure I'd be able to do that without burning the dinner." She went on to explain the pickle her sister had found herself in and took a deep breath, anticipating her friend's response.

"That's no biggie. Sorry, I didn't mean to sound so blasé about it. He's committed fraud, it's as simple as that. We can get the revised deed reversed and kick him out, that's the short answer."

"That's what I thought. Any idea how we can keep this loan shark away from the house in the meantime?"

"Send me his details in the morning, and I'll drop him an email, warning him that we'll take things further if he contacts your sister about this or if he shows up at the house. That type of thing can go one of two ways; either he'll back off and get in touch with his own solicitor to start proceedings against your sister and her fella—yes, she's part of this until his name is off the deeds. Or, he might take umbrage that your sister has contacted a solicitor and turn up at the house to strip out all her possessions."

"What? Oh God, we can't allow that to happen. Lesley has worked hard all her life and put her heart and soul into furnishing that house over the years. She's always saved up to buy anything she wanted, never had anything on finance at all. It seems a shame if that were to happen."

"Like I said, it could come to that, there are no guarantees. Leave it with me. Gotta fly, my steak is ready, and I hate it going over."

"Thanks for talking to me, Cynthia. Enjoy your meal." After ending the call, she leaned back against the sofa and closed her eyes.

Mark woke her a few moments later with a gentle kiss on her forehead.

"Hey, sleepyhead. Do you want some dinner?"

She blinked a few times, trying to focus her tired eyes on his handsome face and reached up to tug his head down to hers. They shared a long kiss until he pulled away from her.

"Dinner," he repeated.

"Sorry, I'm coming now. It's not that I don't appreciate your efforts, I do. I'm feeling drained."

"Have this then go to bed. Listen to your body for a change, Sara."

She grinned. "Sounds like a good idea. You could always join me."

"Cheeky. We'll see."

They ate the delicious meal at the kitchen table. Sara felt less tired after she'd eaten. Together, they tidied up the kitchen while she told Mark about what had occurred at her parents' house with Lesley.

"Wow, I had no idea he could be so devious. Your poor sister."

"I know, I really feel for her. Seventy grand is a mind-blowing amount to be indebted with, isn't it? Shame on him for dragging my sister into this shitty mess. Still, I've done all I can for now. Hopefully Cynthia's intervention will stop this loan shark going after them, at least for now. Enough about them, there's little we can do about it until the morning. Now, weren't we discussing an early night a little while ago?"

4

*M*ie laid on a few nibbles for her pals who were expected at eight p.m. Although she was still feeling the effects of grief, she was willing to set that aside for now to welcome her dear friends. It was to be a casual affair, no posh dresses on show, not tonight. She'd put on a bright-red jumpsuit. Her wardrobe was limited in the black department. She felt red was a far more suitable colour for the occasion. She sniggered and appraised her appearance in the full-length mirror in her bedroom. The view from the side showed off her trim figure. She was sure to attract another man soon, wasn't she? *Do I need another man?*

That was a question she knew would be prominent in her mind for months to come. At present, she felt free for the first time in years. Free and alive, unlike Lens. She paused and studied herself in the mirror. Fine lines appeared at the sides of her eyes, even though she had flawless skin.

A sudden rush of guilt flushed through her. She hadn't had the courage to tell her daughter, Lizzie, about her father's death yet. Maybe an evening with the girls would give her the strength she needed to make the call to Newcastle. Her daughter was close to Lens —wasn't that normal between every father and daughter? Maybe not.

She reconsidered the thought, knowing what some of her friends had gone through during their parents' marriage break-ups when they were all in their teens at school. Her daughter, no doubt, would want to rush home and be with her, cramping her newly found freedom. No, she couldn't tell her yet. Perhaps in a day or two. She realised there would be a backlash to her decision, but she needed this time to herself to grow accustomed to her new life. Anyway, she had a busy few days coming up ahead of her.

The doorbell rang. She ran down the stairs and welcomed her first guest, Jacqueline Beard. A wonderful woman, bright, articulate, a close friend and member of the group who had spent most of their ten years together fighting off the advances of men. Her short blonde hair was never out of place; her frequent visits to the hairdresser saw to that. In her younger days, she'd been a model on the circuit at all the major fashion shows, in high demand by all the big-name designers. That was until she fell in love with Alan Beard.

"Darling, how are you?" Mie pulled Jacqueline into her arms in a much-needed warm embrace.

Jacqueline stepped away from her and smiled. "Hey, I should be the one asking you that? How do you feel?"

"Surprisingly good. A lot better than Lens, let's say that."

They both laughed. "Ouch, you are a scream. I can't wait to hear what went on, can you?"

"I want to know—then again, I don't. I'm sure I'll change my mind once the other girls are here."

The front door opened, and Maria Annibal joined them. Her stunning red hair glistened under the chandelier lights. She'd gone over the top with her makeup as usual, but this was Maria's trait—she had to be the one who stood out in the crowd. She would do that this evening, because in spite of everyone agreeing this would be an informal gathering, Maria was wearing a slinky silver dress that stopped mid-thigh, showing off her slender, shapely legs, that drew plenty of attention from both men and women alike.

Mie and Maria high-fived each other and hugged tightly.

"How are you?" Maria whispered in her ear.

"Thanks to you, I'm fine. Was it hard?"

"Nope. Not when I realised how much that bastard had hurt you."

"He did, there was no denying that. They all have over the years, each and every one of the bastards. Well, no more. By the end of this week, we'll all be free to go on and find a better life, one that each of us is deserving of."

The door eased open behind them, and the final member of the group joined them. Di Powell was the youngest member. She'd been going on about divorcing her husband for years but had never plucked up the courage to go through with it. She had an affinity with Maria who had recently dumped her husband and whose divorce had gone through quickly in comparison. Di's plans to seek the advice of a solicitor were on the backburner. Her husband, Victor, had made her life hell for years, telling her lie after lie about the women whose names he kept in his little black book—the book she'd discovered a few weeks earlier.

"How are you coping, Mie?" Di asked, hugging the girls one by one upon arrival.

"Surprisingly well, I have to say. I feel liberated finally. You'll all experience the same feeling when your time comes. Let's go into the lounge. I've prepared a little buffet for us." Mie grinned like an eight-year-old.

The women nattered excitedly and gasped as soon as they saw the spread Mie had laid on for them.

"You did this all yourself?" Jacqueline asked, clearly mesmerised by the magnificent display.

Mie tilted her head back and laughed. "Hardly. I'm a grieving widow, don't you know. I employed a catering firm I use for entertaining. They came up with this at short notice. Not bad, eh?"

"Wow," Di said, letting out a high-pitched whistle. "Bloody hell, do you do this for everyone? Or only pull out the stops for your deceased cheating husband?"

Mie grinned. "The latter. Although we do tend to give our kinfolks a good send-off back in Denmark, that doesn't usually occur until after the funeral has taken place. Enough chatting, let's start on the champagne."

She sashayed her way to the bar at the far end of the room and popped the cork, much to everyone's excitement. There was something deliciously wicked about the noise. Each of her friends took a filled glass of bubbles from the bar and held it out. "To us, and the freedom that lies ahead of us," Di announced.

The satisfying clink of the glasses filled the room, and then there was silence as the women knocked back their drinks in one go.

Although she finished her drink before everyone else, Mie noticed that Maria, who was standing next to her, wasn't looking as enthusiastic as the others.

Mie nudged her arm and whispered, "Everything all right, sweetie?"

Maria smiled weakly and nodded.

"Come on, you can tell me. What's wrong?" Mie pressed gently.

Maria shrugged. "I'm scared. The deed has been done, and I was very careful, ensured I didn't leave any clues behind for the cops to find, but I'm not feeling elated about my actions. Is that normal?"

"No idea, having never killed a person before," Mie replied, burping slightly after downing her drink too fast. "What do you think, girls? Maria is scared and feeling out of sorts with the situation."

Jacqueline took a few paces towards Maria and placed an arm around her shoulders. "It's natural. The buzz of doing the deed was bound to wear off after a while. You'll get through this. Hey, you're not having second thoughts about your old man, are you?"

Maria's gaze dropped to the inch-thick cream carpet beneath her feet.

Jacqueline squeezed her shoulders. "It's normal for you to be a little down. I think we're all expecting this to hit us in a major way, once we've all completed our part in the scheme. Come on, try and get past this as quickly as you can. Are you sure you want Jack's life to end?"

"Yes and no. Can we talk outside?"

Jacqueline nodded, took hold of Maria's hand and led her outside onto the glamorous patio. The wind had got up and was ruffling the parasol above them as they took a seat.

~

"This is so unlike you, Maria. What's really going on here?"

Maria shrugged. "I wish I knew. Mie seems okay with it all. I suppose I keep thinking how I'm going to be when I hear the news that Jack is dead. He's not really a bad man, not compared to some of the others. I guess I'm asking myself if I have the right to strip him of his life, to play God, if you will."

"Bloody hell, Maria, it's a bit late to be asking yourself that. This has been spoken about and planned out for weeks now. If I recall rightly, you were one of the main instigators. Yes?"

Maria closed her eyes and inhaled a large breath. "It's hard to explain. I never dreamt that I'd have the courage to take another person's life, but let's face it, that's what this amounts to. Did any of us really take that on board in the beginning? Damn, I'm confused. Scared mostly. What if the cops come knocking on my door, demanding to know all sorts? How the heck am I going to pretend I know nothing? I'm not in the habit of lying. Don't they say you have to have an amazing memory to be a liar? My memory is lousy at the best of times. Shit, why did I do it? Listen to me, how selfish I've become in a matter of bloody hours. I should be sitting here grieving the loss of a friend's husband. Instead, I'm trying to figure out how to save my own skin if the cops come calling. That's not natural, is it?"

Jacqueline grasped Maria's hands in her own. "You're right to have these dilemmas running through your head. It's only expected to feel confused when you've just done something out of character. I don't know what the answer is to any of the points you've just raised because I haven't found myself in your position, but by the end of the week, we'll all be in the same boat. You're going to have to take heart from that."

"What if we hate each other at the end of this? What then?"

Jacqueline shrugged and shook her head. "I don't have the answer to that, no one does. I'm presuming there will be lots of discussions like this one, where people's doubts will come to the fore and have to be dealt with. To be brutally honest with you, I couldn't envisage what I was going to feel like. Seeing how this is all affecting you, I have to say it has planted extra doubts in my mind."

"Oh gosh, what if the others say the same? Where will that leave us? Do you think we'll become stronger as a group or will it split us apart?"

"I wish I had a crystal ball to give you an answer to that. The truth is, none of us know."

"God, I hope I don't live to regret this, but I have a feeling I'm going to. Do you think it's too late to back out now?"

Jacqueline frowned. "For you, yes, you've done your part."

"But Mie hasn't killed Jack yet. I could put a stop to that."

"If you go down that route, then every one of us is going to feel the same way. You're only going to make matters worse than they are already. My advice would be to make an appointment with your shrink at the earliest convenience. She'll sort you out. She's always been good for you in the past, hasn't she?"

"What if I blurt out what I've done? No, I can't take the risk. Once I'm lying on that couch of hers, my mouth tends to have a life of its own. I couldn't go there and lie; she'd be able to tell instantly and then she'd work on me. She has a habit of doing that. Oh shit, what a mess."

Jacqueline forced her friend to stand and hugged her. "Talk to me instead of your shrink then and I'll do the same when it comes to my turn. Is that a deal?"

A shuddering sigh left Maria's body. "Deal, I guess. Thanks for the pep talk, sweetie."

"You're welcome. Come on, let's join the others."

They walked back into the lounge to the sound of laughter.

~

*M*ie turned their way. "Hey, what have you two been up to? Is everything okay?"

"Yep, just having a quiet chat. What have we missed, anything?" Jacqueline asked, smiling.

Di went to the bar and topped up their glasses. She handed Jacqueline and Maria theirs and then raised a toast. "To Maria. Who'd have thought that she, the meek and mild one amongst us, would ever have the courage to pull it off?"

The others raised their glasses in her direction and shouted, "To Maria."

With another glass of bubbles downed quickly, everyone made their way over to the large table groaning under the weight of the food. They filled a china plate with everything, from tiny triangle sandwiches of salmon and cream cheese to a collection of tapas dishes.

"Tuck in, darlings, there's more where that came from, and don't start whinging about your diets either. This is a time for celebration, sod everything else. Once we've eaten, I have a surprise to share with you all."

"What's that?" Jacqueline asked.

Mie tapped the side of her nose. "Wait and see." She nibbled on the edge of her sandwich and winked.

The women tucked in, attacking the table's contents as if they hadn't seen any real food for a month. Mie knew they wouldn't be able to resist the temptation once it was laid out in front of them.

Around half an hour later, Mie drew their attention. "I have an announcement to make that I'm sure you'll all be in favour of."

"Go on, stop teasing us," Di shouted.

"Okay, let me finish. I've booked us all a holiday."

The women all stared at each other and gasped.

"Where?" Di was the first to ask.

"I've hired an island, not quite up to Richard Branson's standards, but an island nonetheless. It's in the Caribbean. Girls, I've booked it for a whole month. How's that then?"

"You're amazing, Mie. You didn't have to do that," Jacqueline replied.

"I know I didn't. Call it my gift to us, all of us, for finally having the courage to rid ourselves of these evil men."

"God, I'm in dire need of a holiday," Di said, almost sounding relieved. "When are we due to fly out?"

"In two weeks."

"Wow, you don't hang around, do you?" Jacqueline said, her mouth hanging open for a moment or two.

"Nope, that's how it's going to be from now on with me. No man is ever going to hold me back from doing what I want in the future."

"We'll see about that." Di chuckled. "My bet is that you'll have a younger man servicing you before the month is out."

The group of women laughed at the mortified expression on Mie's face.

"No way. Maybe give me two months to organise that. I'm kidding, seriously, I'm going to sit back and enjoy my freedom for years to come. Yes, I have needs that'll desire servicing now and again. Who says I have to move another fella in to do that? I'll hire a male escort for the evening if I have to. Lord knows I'll have the money to do that once Lens' insurance policy pays out. Of course, I'll have to give Lizzie a share of that..."

"Oh my God, I forgot about Lizzie. What was her reaction when she heard the news about Lens?" Jacqueline asked, taking a sip from her glass.

"Eek... You're all going to hate me now when you hear my answer. The truth is, I haven't plucked up the courage to tell her yet."

"Why?" Di was the first to ask.

"I couldn't bring myself to do it, I thought I'd ring her tomorrow when I'm hungover. Hopefully I'll sound upset to her."

"You're a devious woman, Mie," Jacqueline said.

"Who? Me?" Mie grinned.

Maria was the only one who remained quiet.

It didn't go unnoticed by Mie. "Everything all right, Maria?"

"I suppose so. Jacqueline and I have been having a chat. Truthfully, I'm not sure how I feel at present."

"You'll be fine once the realisation of what just happened wears off."

"I hope so. Enough talk about this wonderful holiday, we need to discuss what's next."

"Let's enjoy ourselves a bit more first, then I'll show you what I have planned for your old fella."

Maria gulped and nodded.

It was a good half an hour before all the women were replete and suitably giggly for Mie to show them what she had in store for Maria's husband, Jack. She instructed her friends to follow her into her office at the top of the stairs. Mie produced the key from her padded bra and flung the door open to reveal an easel on which stood a flip pad. Several chairs had been placed in front of the easel.

"Come in and grab a seat, girls. You'll like this. I've been working secretly on this since our first meeting. It has been extremely hard keeping my mouth shut, I can assure you."

Intrigued, the friends all looked at each other and entered the room. They sat side by side in the seats provided and stared at the setup in front of them.

Once everyone's attention was focused on the chart, Mie flipped over the cover to reveal what she'd come up with to get rid of Jack Annibal. "Welcome to what I have in mind for Jack, ladies."

Her gaze immediately directed to Maria who seemed as though she was about to vomit. Mie reached behind the chart and collected the wastepaper bin from beside her desk. She thrust it on Maria's lap just in time.

Maria heaved into the bin.

Di handed her a clean tissue and rubbed her arm. "Are you all right, sweetheart?"

"I don't know. What is this, Mie, a bomb?"

Mie clapped her friend. "Bravo, you figured it out. Genius, isn't it?"

Jacqueline shook her head in disbelief. "How are you going to bloody achieve that, Mie?"

"I have friends who are willing to help me."

"Are you mad?" Di shouted. "We agreed to keep this between the four of us, no outsiders. You've gone back on that promise. Bloody hell, Mie. You always have to be the odd one out, don't you?"

"Hush now. What difference does it make how we kill them? The aim is to rid ourselves of these monsters and to live our lives as we want."

"The difference is," Jacqueline piped up, "we made a promise. A pact for all of us to adhere to. Involving others carries a risk of getting caught. Have you paid this person or people?"

"I haven't yet but I will. Not much because he owes me a favour," Mie replied, wounded that the other women appeared to be turning on her.

"What kind of favour are we talking about, and how the heck do you broach the subject about using a bomb to blow up a friend's husband?" Di demanded, running a hand through her short hair.

Mie sighed. "Guys, chill, will you? It's all in hand. I assure you, there won't be any comeback on me or anyone else. I trust this guy; he's always been like a brother to me. I can't go into detail. You'll have to take my word that he's an expert in his field and more than willing to do this for me."

Maria shook her head. "You have friends who are damn terrorists? That's what you're saying, aren't you?"

Mie shrugged. "Yes, okay, my secret is out. Damn you all, here's the background I have hidden from you all these years: back in the day, many moons ago, I used to be part of the IRA."

Gasps filled the medium-sized room. "Jesus, this has to be some kind of wind-up," Jacqueline said under her breath.

Mie flopped into a vacant chair and placed her elbows on her knees, her gaze drifting between them. "No. Both Lens and I used to be active members. That's what initially brought us to the UK."

"Goodness me, or words to that effect. I'm not sure I can deal with this," Di said, shaking her head slowly.

"Mie, after all these years, why haven't you confided in us?" Jacqueline appeared hurt by the revelation, and this pulled on Mie's heartstrings.

"Girls, I sense you turning on me. Please don't do this. All the IRA stuff was in my past."

"Then leave it there. Why call on your former associates to do this for you?" Di jumped in.

"I saw the opportunity to make an impact and seized it. Maria, you haven't said anything. You agree with this, don't you?"

Maria shook her head. "No. I can't let Jack go in this manner. Are you crazy?" She left her chair and paced the room, touching her face nervously.

"Chill, all of you. It's too late to prevent this now. It has to go ahead. It's due to happen in the next day or so."

"No!" Maria shouted, tears streaming down her cheeks. "You have to stop it, or I'll go to the police and confess everything."

"You'll do no such thing, Maria. We made a pact, we have to stick to that," Di reprimanded her in a headmistress's tone.

Maria flung herself into her chair and buried her head in her hands.

Jacqueline comforted her dear friend. "Take a breath, love. It's true, we made a pact, and each of us has a job to do. You're feeling raw at present, numb by what you did to Lens, no doubt."

"You're right. But...I can't let Jack go out like this."

Jacqueline sighed and stared at Mie. "She's right, no one signed up for anything as gruesome as this, Mie. You'll have to think up something else."

"I won't do it. Listen to me, this is the best way, I promise you. Jack won't have a clue what's hit him. He'll die instantly. Unlike Lens. My betting is that he was scared witless, am I right, Maria?"

Maria nodded her acceptance of the statement. "You are. He was scared. So was I all the time I was bashing his brains in. But this?" She pointed at the detailed account of what lay ahead on the chart.

"The key is not to think about it," Mie said. "Maybe it was wrong of me to reveal my plans to you all. I'm begging you not to think badly of me. I'd die of loneliness if you lot ditched me as your friend."

"We won't," Jacqueline replied. "All this has come as a shock though. Surely you can see that?"

"I can. I'm sorry. I was going to go through everything step by step but I fear it'll only make things a darn sight worse. Come, let's go back downstairs, put some music on and have a party."

Di shook her head and stood. "I can't do this."

"Do what?" Mie bit back.

"Any of it. It's warped. I mean, why go after Maria's husband anyway when she's divorced?"

"Jesus, do we have to keep going over this? He wronged her, left her distraught and destitute while he lives in a mansion with his secretary who is twenty years his junior. Is that right in your eyes?"

Di shrugged. "Maria will find someone new one day. She's rid of him; he's someone else's problem."

"That's unfair on Maria," Jacqueline said, jumping out of her chair. "She's the only one who has had the courage to do the deed. Do you think that was easy for her? No, look at her. She's torn up inside. She deserves her moment of glory just like the rest of us. So what if she's divorced, what the hell does that matter? He deserves all that's coming to him and more besides for the way he shat on her."

Maria smiled and reached for Jacqueline's hand. "Thank you for sticking up for me, you wonderful woman. Maybe things have got a little out of hand emotionally."

"They have," Mie agreed. "Let's go back downstairs and forget about this for now."

"We still have to decide if we're going to go ahead with our pact or not," Di insisted. "If we've all got cold feet then we should surely knock things on the head for now."

"I said, leave the discussion for now. I want to party." Mie flounced out of the room and waited on the landing for everyone else to join her then locked it again and replaced the key in her bra.

She skipped down the stairs ahead of her friends and had poured out four glasses of champagne by the time everyone entered the lounge. "Cheers, here's to our long-standing friendship. We've encountered far worse things over the years and always stuck together. May our friendship survive what lies ahead of us and go from strength to strength in years to come. I love you, girls."

She clinked the edge of each of her friends' glasses and gulped down her bubbles in one go. The others shrugged and did the same.

The evening swung into action after that. They picked at the remainder of the food and boogied the night away, all their fears and concerns pushed aside for the time being.

In a quieter moment, Mie took Maria to one side, gave her a hug and asked, "Is everything all right between us? I would hate for any of this to ruin our fabulous friendship, sweetheart."

"It's all right. I didn't mean to sound off upstairs. I was shocked, that's all."

"And now?" Mie asked, hopefully.

"I've come to terms with it. Do what you have to do, Mie. That was the idea in the first place, to rid ourselves of these men who have wronged us," Maria replied, a weak smile on her lips.

"You're amazing. You won't regret this."

"When is it going to happen?" Maria asked quietly.

Mie hesitated. "You really want to know? What if you have a change of heart overnight and phone him?"

"I won't, I promise."

"Okay, tomorrow. My guy has been following him around all week. Jack has a routine he sticks to, so he thinks it'll be easy to do what's necessary tomorrow."

"Ah, yes, Jack was always a creature of habit." Maria giggled. "I'm glad it's going to prove to be his downfall. It used to drive me nuts."

They both laughed. Di and Jacqueline turned to look their way.

Mie raised her glass at them. "To us. To our much-anticipated freedom."

"To us," the other three women shouted, clinking their glasses together.

5

*S*ara ran through her proposed agenda in the car on the way into work that morning, cursing as she arrived at the Roman Road roundabout to find the traffic ground to a halt. *Why, oh why, did I have that extra cuddle with Mark this morning?* She smiled, thinking the experience had been worth it. Not for the first time on days like today, she thought how lucky she was to have him in her life. Now, they were settled and their recent troubles were behind them, she had realised he meant as much to her as Philip had, if not more. Mark was one in a million. Kind, gentle, compassionate, and a tower of strength when he needed to be. She knew he'd never set out to hurt her, not intentionally, and the added bonus was that her parents loved him as much as she did.

Carla was waiting for her in the station's car park when she arrived.

"I know, I'm late. Damn traffic. You could have gone on ahead. Is everything all right?"

"I thought you usually left early to avoid getting caught up? Yes, I'm fine."

"Try telling your face that," Sara said, tilting her head and smiling.

"Don't start on me. I've barely slept all night."

Sara opened the door to the main entrance, and they walked up the stairs together.

"Any reason?"

"It's just this damn feeling niggling away at me that something is about to go wrong. I know, I sound like the voice of doom when I should be filled with happiness and fairy dust."

"You're going to have to try and push that feeling aside, Carla, and get on with your life. You have a decent man now who is hopefully treating you well, unlike the previous bastard who needed his dick chopped off. Push through this and let the happiness take over."

Carla chortled. "You make me laugh with the things that come out of your mouth when I least expect them to."

"I like to keep people on their toes. You all think you know me. Christ, I don't even know myself or what's going to come out of my own mouth at times."

Carla's face cracked for the first time. "I love working with you, umm...most of the time."

"And the rest of the time?"

Carla held her hand up and waved it from side to side. "That's debatable."

"Charming."

They entered the incident room to find everyone else at their desks, heads down, beavering away.

"Morning, all. Everyone all right this morning?"

The team members either nodded or raised a thumb in the air.

Sara breezed into her office to survey what the internal post had brought her. Thankfully, the pile was much smaller than usual. She sat at her desk and got stuck in straight away. Carla surprised her with a cup of coffee which helped keep the boredom levels at bay. An hour passed, and she returned to the outer office and circulated her team.

"Anything interesting shown up on our victim as yet?" she asked DS Jill Smalling.

"Nothing as yet, boss. Only what we found yesterday about him coming over to settle in the UK twenty years ago. I'm still trying to come up with something new."

"Okay, don't stress about it. Carla and I are going to visit the wife now. Hopefully she'll be more receptive to us today. Of course, that could go belly up and she might slam the door in our faces when we get there."

"I hope she can give you some kind of lead to go on, because we're struggling so far. We hate to let you down like this."

Sara placed a hand on her shoulder. "Nonsense, you guys could never let me down. If there are no clues to be had, then we'll keep digging until we find some. I have faith in you all, always have had."

Jill's cheeks flushed with colour. "Thanks. That means a lot."

"Carla, are you ready to go?"

Her partner left her chair and slipped on her black jacket. Sara collected hers, and they set off. The journey was less fraught than Sara's previous one that morning.

They drew up outside Mie Jensen's magnificent home around fifteen minutes later.

"Ugh, the curtains are still drawn upstairs. I hope this isn't going to turn out to be a wasted trip," Sara noted.

"Me, too. Maybe it's a Danish custom. Didn't folks used to draw their curtains when someone had died in the family in the UK years ago?"

"Possibly. Not sure how you expect me to remember that. I'm not that much older than you, cheeky mare."

Carla cringed. "I wasn't trying to cause offence or be funny…"

"Chill, I was winding you up. I'm not really up to scratch on quaint English traditions. I'll make a note to ask my mum later, she'll know."

They exited the vehicle, and Sara rang the ornate bell on the right of the front door. It was a while before Mie Jensen appeared. She looked rough, as if they'd interrupted her sleep. Her previous day's makeup was still in place but heavily smudged around the eyes. Sara shuddered at the thought of wearing all her makeup to bed, not that she wore that much on a daily basis anyway.

"Yes, what do you want?" She peered at them and then blinked a few times as though her eyes were still adjusting to the daylight.

"Hello, Mie. As promised, we've come back to see you. To ask you a few questions if you're up to it?"

"Oh God, did I really agree to this? I'm in no fit state to see anyone this morning. You'll have to call back another time, when it's more convenient."

"Ordinarily, we would, except this is a murder enquiry, and I must insist you talk to us ASAP. We did the right thing giving you a wide berth yesterday, to allow you to grieve a little."

Her eyes narrowed, and she glared at Sara. "You're delusional if you believe the grieving process only takes twenty-four hours, lady."

"Sorry, I didn't mean it to sound like that. Of course it's going to take you longer than that to come to terms with your husband's death. Please, why don't you give us half an hour of your time today and then boot us out? Without hearing any facts about your husband, the case will take longer to solve. That won't be good for either of us, will it?"

She heaved out a sigh and rested her head against the door. "I'll need a pint of coffee before I answer any of your questions."

Sara smiled, her objective to put the woman at ease. "Sounds good to me. We'd love one, if you're offering."

Mie adjusted her position and stood behind the door to allow them access. They walked past the lounge, and Mie hurriedly closed the door to the room. Fortunately, Sara had already noticed the mess in the room. Which raised her suspicions. Evidence of a party rather than a grieving wife looking for solace in the bottom of a bottle. Mie walked ahead of them, swaying from side to side as she went.

Sara nudged Carla and mouthed, "She's hungover, not grieving."

Carla's eyes widened. "Really?" she mouthed back.

Sara nodded, anger building inside and flowing through her system. She needed to calm down, reminding herself that the woman was Danish and that she was unaware of their customs surrounding a loved one's death. She'd give the woman the benefit of the doubt for now, she had to.

Sara and Carla made themselves comfortable on the stools at the island and watched Mie work her magic with the coffee machine, except the process wasn't as smooth as it had been the day before. She spilt most of the coffee on the counter, cursing herself as she wiped up the mess and threw the cloth in the bin. She started over and achieved her aim the second time around, much to everyone's relief.

"Sorry, it's been a rough night. I slept deeper than I anticipated."

"No need to make excuses, we totally understand. Did you manage to contact your family all right yesterday?"

Mie appeared to hesitate. Sara could tell she was wracking her brain for the conversation they'd held the previous day.

"Ah yes, it was an all-day job. They asked when the funeral was likely to be. I said that I'd ask you guys and get back to them. Any idea?"

"It depends on the pathologist's findings and whether she's ready to release the body. I'm sorry to have to tell you that in cases where murder is suspected, then the likelihood of releasing the body early isn't very likely."

"What? Why?"

"Sometimes, as the information we gather comes in, we find it necessary to do further tests on the body."

"I don't understand. Are you saying the tests the pathologist does initially aren't always precise?"

"No, they're accurate enough, it's just that certain proof might arise later. If the body was released to the family early and they proceeded with the funeral, well, let's say that could cause unnecessary bad feelings with the next of kin."

"Ah, I think I understand. Thank God the coffee is ready." Mie poured three cups of strong coffee and handed them around. She offered Sara and Carla some milk but chose to drink hers black. "Have you found the person responsible for my husband's death?"

"Not yet. At present we have virtually nothing to go on. No evidence found at the scene. That in itself will always put a major dent in an investigation. Hence our need to speak with you at the earliest convenience."

Mie swallowed. "I'm sorry. I feel guilty now for dismissing you yesterday. Maybe you should have insisted and pushed me for answers."

"That's not how we prefer to do things, Mie. We appreciate people have to get used to the idea of losing a loved one, especially where a spouse is concerned. If you're up to answering a few questions now, it'll go a long way to helping us with our enquiries."

"I can't promise you that I will have all the answers you're seeking but I will certainly do my best to help you. What do you need to know?"

"First of all, Andy Lockwood gave us a few names of your husband's competitors yesterday. We contacted them, and they were all shocked and horrified to learn of your husband's death."

"Really? And you believed them?"

"We have no reason to disbelieve them. We might revisit the situation later on in the investigation if something else comes to light. Can you think of any reason why someone would want to hurt Lens?"

"No, none whatsoever. He went about his business like any other businessman I know. Worked exceptionally long hours to provide for his family."

"Do you have any children, Mie?"

Mie stared at the coffee cup nestled in her hands and nodded. "Our daughter, Lizzie. She's eighteen and at university in Newcastle."

"I guess she'll be coming home in the next day or two to be with you?"

"I suppose so. I haven't plucked up the courage to tell her yet. She was very close to her father. I guess I'm struggling to find the right words. It's not really something you should tell your daughter over the phone, I'm sure you'll agree."

"I do. Perhaps it might be worth catching a train or taking a flight up to see her. I'm sure she'd want to know first-hand rather than hear it mentioned on the news."

"Oh gosh, the news. I never even thought about that. How silly of me. I'll correct that when you have gone. I'll call her and share the terrible news. Wait, she's going to be devastated. Maybe I should reconsider and go up there instead. You see, the decisions I've had to make and continue to make aren't easy at all, not when your family is spread miles apart, even countries apart as with our parents and siblings. I had an horrendous day yesterday."

"I can imagine. I'm sure your friends rallied around to ease your pain, yes?"

Mie glanced up and frowned. "I'm not with you, Inspector."

"The mess in the lounge. Surely you didn't make that all yourself last night?"

Mie gulped and shook her head. "Yes, I can't deny it. My friends who are closest to me came over and insisted on bringing some food with them. In the end, we treated the evening as a celebration for my husband's life. Is there something wrong with that?"

"No, not at all. In the UK, that kind of tradition usually happens after the deceased has been buried or cremated."

"It wasn't a wake. It was an impromptu soirée, if you will. My friends looking out for me, ensuring that I ate properly."

"And had enough fluids, too, I should imagine."

Mie's face turned a dark shade of red, and she blustered, "Yes, there was alcohol consumed. I hope your detective skills will prove to be as efficient going forward, Inspector, in your search for my husband's killer."

"I'm sure they will. There's not a lot that gets past me, Mie," Sara replied, puffing out her chest proudly.

Carla nudged her leg underneath the lip of the island.

"I'm glad to have such a qualified and competent police officer and her team on my husband's case. It's a relief also."

"I hope we don't let you down. Okay, going back to possible motives for your husband's death. Going back to our last visit, I asked if you would give us a list of your husband's friends who we could have a chat with."

"I could. May I ask why?"

"At the moment, we have very little to go on. As you can appreciate, the more people we can interview who knew your husband, the better. Maybe they can give us some information that you don't know about."

"Are you telling me that you think my husband had secrets that I'm unaware of?"

Sara thought back to the conversation she'd had with Jensen's work colleague who had highlighted the man's penchant for young ladies. "Possibly. It wouldn't be the first time we've come across something like that during an investigation. I'm sure there's nothing for you to worry about. It's better for us to err on the side of caution."

Mie nodded. "I understand. I hope you don't find anything. In my eyes, my husband was perfect." Again, another blush developed in her cheeks, and her gaze dropped to her cup.

"Glad to hear it. Maybe your husband's death was a spur of the moment thing for the killer. We've yet to establish that or a possible motive. I'm sure you can understand how difficult an investigation is with minimal evidence or clues at our disposal."

"I do. I hope something comes your way soon. Let me try and get the information for you. I'll need to go into my husband's study; all his contact information is in there. We're lucky; he preferred to use a Rolodex system, always said he needed a backup plan in case either his phone or computer ceased to work." She hopped off the stool, taking her cup of coffee with her.

Once she'd left the room, Sara turned to peek over her shoulder to ensure the woman was out of earshot. "What do you think?"

"About what?" Carla asked, looking perplexed.

Sara scratched the side of her head. "Is it just me who is getting a bad vibe from this?"

"I'm not getting a bad vibe at all. The woman is mourning the loss of her husband, give her a break."

Sara thought back to the days immediately after her own husband's death and shook her head. She lowered her voice, "When Philip passed away, I was like a zombie for a good few weeks."

"Stop right there. You can't think negatively about her reactions. For a start, she's a foreigner—that has to count for something, doesn't it?"

"You think? Why?"

Carla shrugged and pulled a face. "Ask me another. I don't know, possibly in their country they deal with death differently."

Sara nodded. "Okay, we need to research that side of things when we get back to the station. All right, answer me this then: why hasn't she told her daughter?"

Carla let out an exasperated sigh. "She told you why. She doesn't want to tell her that type of thing over the phone. Think about it, would you want to hear something like that during a phone conversation?"

"Ugh...I'll give you that one. And thirdly, what about the party she held last night? That's bang out of order in the circumstances."

"God, you're impossible. Think about this logically. All that's happened is her friends have rallied around, supplied her with food that she wouldn't want to prepare for herself at such a sad time."

"I repeat, when I lost Philip, the last thing on my mind was having a shindig with my friends. I went into my shell, did everything I could to shut everyone out. That included my family and especially my work colleagues and friends."

Carla's mouth twitched, the way it always did when she was annoyed with Sara. "And I *repeat*, everybody deals with grief differently. Rather than cast aspersions, why don't we accept that for now?"

They heard Mie on her way back and sipped at their coffees.

Mie entered the room and slid a sheet of paper in front of Sara. "Those are three of his closest friends. I hope their addresses are up to date. Knowing how fastidious Lens was, I'm sure they will be. If not, I'm sure you'll be able to track them down through your system."

"We will, thank you, that's most kind of you."

"Now, if there's nothing else, I need to get ready. I've decided to fly up to Newcastle to visit my daughter and give her the news in person."

"Of course, I think you're making the right decision, Mie. Thank you for the information. Hopefully, something his friends might tell us will prove beneficial to the investigation and enable us to track down the murderer within a few days."

"And if nothing comes of it?"

"I'm due to put out a press conference soon. We're in the process of organising that now. Although the house-to-house enquiries have come back negative so far, it's a dog-walking area, so there might be someone out there who saw something that will prove to be important to us. We live in hope. Have a safe trip; we'll be in touch soon."

"Thank you." Mie saw them out, smiled awkwardly and closed the door behind them.

"Where are we going now?" Carla asked.

"The first friend on our list. Dick Felix." Sara unlocked the car, slid into the driver's seat and punched the address into the satnav. "Nearly thirty minutes away. Let me see if either of the other men is closer."

"Can I stop you right there."

Sara turned to look at her partner. "What's wrong?"

"The time of day. Are these men likely to be at home, given they're all businessmen?"

"Crap, you're right. It's almost twelve-thirty. Why don't we find a café or something and have some lunch. We'll ring the station, get one of the guys there to search for the information we need and start again after we've eaten."

"Sounds good. I'll get on to Christine."

Sara started the engine and pulled up the local area on her phone's map. It highlighted a café a few minutes' drive from the house.

By the time Sara had found a spare parking space close to the small café, Carla had instructed Christine on what she needed and also told the rest of the team to pause for a bit to have some lunch.

Inside the clean but small café, the tables were close together. Only a few of them were occupied.

"I fancy a bacon roll, what do you want? I'm paying."

"You always pay. I'll shout us this one," Carla insisted.

She swept past Sara to speak to the petite blonde woman who was waiting to take their order behind the counter. Her hair was tied back in a ponytail. There was a man in chef's whites flipping burgers and sausages on the grill behind her.

"Can I get two bacon rolls and two white coffees, please?"

"Sure. Why don't you find a table and I'll bring it over to you?" the young woman replied in a cheery voice.

Sara chose a table at the rear, and they wound their way through the other customers. While they waited, Sara told Carla what had happened the previous evening.

"It's been a hectic morning. I forgot to tell you last night my sister and I met up at my parents' house. She wasn't happy."

The waitress appeared with their coffees. "Five minutes on the rolls, ladies."

"No problem," Carla said, smiling. She turned her attention back to Sara. "Go on."

"Well, she told us the wedding was off. I told you she was getting married, didn't I?"

"I seem to remember you saying something along those lines. Can I ask why?"

"He's in debt up to his eyeballs and has now dragged her into it."

"Damn, how?"

"He's forged her signature on the deeds to the house."

"The bastard. I hope you're gonna throw the book at him?"

"I'm doing all I can. I rang a solicitor friend of mine last night when I eventually got home. She's going to get something done about it. This could cost a lot in bloody legal fees."

"Does that matter? Surely your sister can use the funds she set aside for the wedding to pay any likely fees."

"I suppose so. My parents said they'd chip in as well. The prat is refusing to move out, and there's the threat of this loan shark laying heavy on her. Lesley was in a right state last night. I accompanied her home and threatened him, that's all I could do. It won't stop me damn well worrying about her, though."

"Bloody hell, what a damn cheek. Can I ask how much debt this tosser is in?"

"To the tune of seventy grand."

Carla whistled. "Shit, that's horrendous. No wonder your sister is beside herself. Is the house hers? Of course it is, otherwise he wouldn't have forged his signature on the deeds."

"Exactly. She bought the house before she ever got involved with him. I feel so sorry for her. I've never liked Brendan, there's always been something niggling about him. If I was allowed to do a background check on him at work, I would have done it years ago. I value my job, though, and you know what happens if you're caught."

"Yep, definitely not worth the risk. There are other ways of getting the bastard, you know that as well as I do. Between us, we could make his life hell. If that's what you want, you only have to say the word."

The waitress placed a huge roll in front of each of them. "Enjoy. I bet you don't eat it all. Most people struggle."

"You could have warned us," Sara said, smiling. "We could have had half each."

The waitress winked. "You'll know the next time you drop in. You'll be back, I guarantee it."

They all laughed. It was a brief respite to the serious situation she and Carla had been discussing.

They both took a bite out of their roll. It had three rashers of bacon stuffed inside.

Sara slathered hers with ketchup. "Let me consider the reprisals. Thinking about it, we could pick him up for speeding or driving around on dodgy tyres."

"That's the very least we can do." Carla grinned, taking a huge bite out of her roll, the brown sauce slipping out of the side and landing on her chin.

Sara handed Carla a serviette which she gratefully used to tidy herself up.

Once they'd struggled to eat their lunch—the waitress had been right, neither of them cleared their plates—they left the café with the promise they'd return soon and jumped back in the car. Carla chased Christine for the information and punched in the first postcode. Sara drove to the address which happened to be a solicitor's in the centre of town. She found a free space around fifty yards from the office, and together they walked back, grateful to not be scrunched up in the car after their huge lunch.

They entered the reception area to find several people sitting in the waiting area. Sara's heart sank; she anticipated a long delay to see the man they had come to visit. Sara flashed her warrant card at the middle-aged receptionist who lifted her glasses to read it.

"Oh my, what can I do for you, ladies?"

"We'd like to see Dick Felix, if that's possible. Urgently," Sara added, hoping to jump ahead of the queue.

"Mr Felix is busy with a client at present, and then he has two more clients to see within the next half an hour. I can make an appointment for later on this afternoon, if that will help?"

Sara wondered if the woman had comprehended the word *urgently*. "We need to see him as soon as possible. We're conducting a murder enquiry."

"Gosh, well, that certainly throws a different light on things. Let me see what I can do for you."

A man sitting by the door shouted, "Don't even think about rear-ranging my appointment. Some of us have a job to go back to. This is my lunch hour I'm wasting here."

The other man sitting a few chairs away nodded. "Ditto. My time's valuable as well."

Sara sighed. She could tell she wasn't about to get anywhere fast and backtracked. "We'll take the appointment later on today. What time would that be?"

"I have four o'clock or four-thirty slots available at the moment. Would either of those do you?"

"Four o'clock would be great. We have a few other people to see in the meantime. See you later." She nodded at the receptionist who jotted down a note in her diary and then smiled at the two men waiting to be seen.

They both grinned at her.

She nodded back at them. "Thanks for your understanding, gents. I hope neither of you needs police assistance any time soon."

Their faces were a picture.

Carla sniggered as she closed the door behind them. "Idiots. I wonder why they were there."

"I bet we'll see them at the cop shop in the near future. Good job I have an excellent memory. I'll be on the lookout for the buggers, don't you worry. Right, we have three hours to fill before we return. Who's next on the list?"

"Ray Carmel. He owns a posh gents' clothing shop in the town centre."

"I never knew such a thing existed. Okay, which way? Shall we venture in by foot?"

"It might be worth sticking a note on the car in case we go over the time limit. You know how pernickety the wardens can be in Hereford."

"Are there any? I don't think I've ever clocked one in the two years I've worked here."

"They're around. They'll probably pounce when you least expect them. I'll stick one in the car now."

Sara pressed the key fob, and the door clunked open. Carla scribbled a note, slapped it on the dashboard and shut the door again. With the vehicle locked, they set off. The shop they were on the lookout for was at the other end of the town.

"Crap, I'm beginning to regret not bringing the car," Sara said. "Not that I'm lazy or anything, but because of the time factor. The last thing we want to do is rush the interviews."

"Shit happens," Carla replied unhelpfully.

The menswear shop was down a small alley and proved difficult to find. Sara had asked several passers-by if they knew the shop. The last person had managed to point them in the right direction. They entered the front door, and an old-fashioned bell tinkled, announcing their arrival.

A man with black hair, showing signs of ageing at the sides, instantly appeared. "Good afternoon, ladies. How may I help you on this cold, damp day?"

Sara hadn't had time to consider what the weather was like outside. She turned to see the rain-slicked pavements scattered with drying patches. Facing the gentleman, she asked, "Would you be Mr Carmel?"

The man frowned. "That's right. And you are?"

"The police. DI Sara Ramsey, and my partner, DS Carla Jameson. Do you have five minutes spare for a chat?" Sara glanced around at the empty shop.

"As it happens, I do. One of my regulars is due in half an hour for a fitting. Would you like to come through to my office? I suppose I should ask what this is all about."

"We're conducting a murder enquiry. Yes, lead the way, sir."

His eyes bulged. "What does this have to do with me?"

"We'll tell you in a moment, sir."

He led the way through a beaded curtain and up a narrow corridor to an office at the rear of the property. The desk was tidy, and the rest of the room was cluttered even though everything appeared to be in its place. Sara acknowledged it was one of the cleanest offices she'd visited in a long, long time.

"Take a seat," he gestured, sitting in his plush chair behind the desk. "Now, what's this all about? Wait, can I stop you right there? If the bell goes, I'll have to shoot out. I'm alone at the moment; my assistant is on her lunchbreak."

"We understand. Perhaps you can tell us how you know a Lens Jensen?"

"He's a close friend of mine. There are four of us who meet up when we can. Why?"

Carla took notes. "When was the last time you saw him, sir?"

"About a week ago. We've all been rather busy lately, so our meetings have had to be set aside for now. Why? What's this about? Has Lens done something illegal?"

"No, not as far as we know. Has Mrs Jensen not contacted you?"

"Mie? Why would she? We meet up at social gatherings, but apart from that we have very little to do with each other. I'm getting the impression that something serious has happened. What is it?"

Sara sighed. "Mr Jensen was found murdered yesterday morning."

He swallowed and shook his head slowly as he digested the news. "No! Not Lens. There must be some mistake."

"No mistake, sir. It has been confirmed. Were you close enough to Lens for him to confide in you?"

"Yes, we confided in each other. We all did. What are you getting at? Oh shit! Wait, I need to let this sink in. Bloody hell! This is... murdered, you say? Why?"

"We've yet to establish a motive, hence our need to track down his friends. We're hoping you can shed some light on that for us?"

"Me? How? This is all news to me. Was he targeted on purpose?" He shook his head in disbelief.

"We're unsure about that yet, sir."

"I really don't know what I can tell you, Inspector. Apart from Lens was a decent enough man."

"Maybe you can recall him telling you if he was having problems at work or in his personal life over the past few months?"

Carmel chewed on his bottom lip as he thought, his gaze drifting out to the window on the left that had a view of a brick wall. He let out a huge breath. "Nothing is coming to mind. I promise you, I would tell you if anything was there."

"What about his penchant for the ladies?"

He chewed his lip harder this time. "You know about that?"

Sara nodded. "One of his colleagues at the haulage firm mentioned it should be something we look into. As you're a close friend, maybe you can enlighten us further."

"Lens was Lens, he liked the ladies. He was Danish. I think you'll find they have a free will where love and sex are concerned."

"Do you know if his wife was aware of this?"

"I don't think so," he started saying then paused and corrected himself, "who can tell? He always told us that he hid it well from her. I think he was delusional. My wife would know the instant I bloody laid eyes on another woman, let alone slept with one."

"Did he have many sexual encounters with women?"

"I'm not sure."

"Honestly, Mr Carmel. We're seeking the truth. There's no point covering up for him, not now your friend is lying in a morgue."

He leaned back in his chair and linked his hands together over his taut stomach. "The truth is, I really can't tell you how many women he had on the go. He saw them at all hours of the day. Mostly during the day when he should have been working. He gave Mie the impression that he worked very long hours. He didn't. His business usually ran itself; he employed excellent staff, paid them well so he could fulfil his needs, if you get my drift."

"Mie must have known about this. If you're trying to pass it off as a Danish trait, then she must have known what he was like."

"Your guess is as good as mine. I take it you've spoken to her?"

"Yes, yesterday and today. She was the one who gave us your name, along with the other two men in your group."

"How is she?"

"Bearing up. When we left her earlier, she was about to fly north to Newcastle to visit their daughter. She hasn't told her yet; she didn't want to do it over the phone."

"Understandable. Lizzie will be shocked. She loved her father."

"It won't be an easy time for either of them. Going back to these women he was cheating on Mie with, I don't suppose you can tell me any names?"

He shook his head. "Sorry, no. There were too many to keep track of."

"He sounds a nice man," Sara replied sarcastically.

Carmel sat upright and pulled back his shoulders. "I won't have you saying anything bad about him. He was an exceptional friend of mine."

"Who cheated frequently on his wife. He sounds a right charmer to me." She grinned tautly at the man. Sensing they weren't going to find out anything more useful, she drew the meeting to a close. "Here's one of my cards. If you can look past all the glowing traits you believe Lens had and remember anything you think we should know about, please get in touch with me right away."

"I will. You can see yourselves out." He remained seated, his features contorted with anger.

Sara and Carla left the office and made their way back through to the shop.

Once they were outside and walking back to the car, Carla tugged on Sara's sleeve to slow her down. "Hey, what's the rush, and why were you so harsh back there?"

Sara eased her pace to near normal. "Guys like Lens piss me off.

Womanising shits, intent on screwing up several people's lives just for an easy lay. Well, it's come back to haunt him, so to speak."

"While I agree with that sentiment, you're forgetting one thing."

"I am? And what's that?"

"This could have been a random attack."

Sara raised her eyebrows at her partner. "The more I hear, the more I'm inclined to disbelieve that angle. I know I shouldn't have snapped back there, but it boils my blood, especially when men like Carmel see their friend's infidelity as a badge of honour. At least that's how it came across to me."

"Not sure I picked up on that."

"Are you saying I was wrong to react that way? Come on, Carla, be honest with me?"

"No. I would never dream of telling you how to conduct an investigation."

"Good. Then why do I sense a 'but' coming?"

Carla shrugged and strode ahead of her. "Just a simple observation that I think we should proceed with an open mind."

Sara caught up with her. "I agree. And you're right to reprimand me."

Carla turned and smiled at her. "I wasn't aware that I had."

"You did. Okay, we have one more to see before we need to head back to the solicitor's office for our appointment."

6

---

*T*he Razzamatazz nightclub was situated on the edge of town. Sara had a feeling the visit would be a wasted trip, given the time of day and the likelihood of anybody being at the club mid-afternoon. She was wrong. The front door was open when she tried it. They entered the old stone building which used to be a former church and walked through the opulent reception area that led to the huge bar and dance floor.

Sara suddenly felt old. It had been years since she'd ventured into a nightclub. This one looked as though it had received a recent makeover. Dotted around the edge of the shiny, wooden dance floor were metal poles. *Are they for the staff or the punters to use?*

"Can I help you, ladies?" A man appeared behind the bar, obviously stocking up the shelves for the night ahead.

"We're looking for Barry Normont."

The man wiped his hands on a bar towel. "You've found him. What can I do for you? If you're after a job, I'd have to turn you down."

"May I ask why?" Sara asked, intrigued.

"No offence, but you're kind of old for this lark, doll."

Sara produced her warrant card. "It's a good job we're suitably employed at present then, isn't it? DI Sara Ramsey, and my partner, DS Carla Jameson."

"Shit! Me and my big mouth. Sorry, I'm always putting my size tens in it."

Sara smiled. "You're forgiven. Let's just say you owe us one."

"Fair enough. What's up?"

Sara glanced around to see if there were any other members of staff in the area. "Are you alone?"

"Yep, I find I think better when I'm bottling up. Just because we don't open until nine this evening, there's still a lot of preparation to be completed before we let the punters run loose around here. I don't recall doing anything against the law. Have I?"

"Not that we're aware of. We're here to ask you a few questions about a friend of yours, a Lens Jensen."

"I see. And what may I ask has he got himself involved in?"

"Nothing, apart from becoming a victim of a serious crime."

He frowned and walked towards the bar where he rested his forearms. "Is he all right?"

"Not really. He was murdered yesterday. I take it you weren't aware of the incident?"

"What? Fuck! How? Where? And no, I wasn't aware. Should I have been?"

Sara shrugged. "We thought the four of you were close and anticipated either the jungle drums or Mie Jensen herself would have shared the news by now."

"Well, they haven't. Maybe they're all reeling from the shock, like I am. Jesus, he didn't deserve to go so young."

"He was in his forties, I believe?"

"He celebrated his forty-second birthday here a few weeks ago."

"Did his family attend? By that, I mean his wife."

"No, not even sure if she was invited. He had his own set of friends, if you get my meaning?"

"As in, the female variety?"

He laughed. "There are no flies on you, Inspector."

"I like to think so. These women, how many? How often? And did any of them turn into a lasting relationship? I'm guessing that he met most of these women here?"

"He did. Occasionally I would introduce him to someone new. He'd come here at night and be surrounded by a bevy of beauties."

"And the women were all right with that sort of behaviour?"

His mouth turned down at the sides. "Yes, there was no reason for them not to be okay with it."

"Sorry, am I missing something? What are you saying?"

"He was in the habit of flashing his cash. Women tend to deal with rich men differently. Are you getting my drift now?"

"Ah, I see. Was there any type of trouble between either of the parties?"

"Not that I could tell. Once these girls latch on to a bloke, that's it really. Anything goes."

"I'm not with you. Anything goes?"

"Onesomes, twosomes, threesomes, more than that even. Lens adored these women and spent most of his time pleasing them, either by spending his money on them or taking them to bed."

Sara shook her head and puffed out her cheeks. The more she learnt about Mr Jensen, the more she disliked him and felt sorry for his wife. Maybe it was the relief that drove her to celebrate his death at the party.

"These girls, were any of them involved with other men, either here at the club or outside, do you know?"

"I only ever introduced him to girls I knew were single. Who's to say if they were telling me the truth or not? You think one of these girls killed him?"

"We're not sure. All we're doing is gathering as much information as we can right now. Hopefully, the pieces will slot together soon and lead us to the perpetrator. Where did Lens bed his lady friends, any idea?"

"I'm presuming at a local hotel. I think he was too tight to rent a nearby flat somewhere. You find that with some rich folks. He might splash his dosh around here to attract the bitches—sorry, the ladies— but once he's ensnared them…"

"Okay, moving on... Did Lens ever have any kind of run-in with any of the other punters? Maybe someone who was jealous of him getting all the attention from these women?"

He thought over the question for a moment or two. "Can't remember anything like that. I caught a few of the male members giving him the evil eye now and again but brushed it off as envy, nothing more. I can't say any one of them would be capable of murdering Lens. Damn, I don't think it has sunk in yet. He was one of my regulars, always here when I needed a chat about the business. He was the one who guided me through the renovations for this place. It was his suggestion to employ the pole dancers. They've been a massive hit so far, too. I'll be forever in his debt." He glanced at the sparkly ceiling. "Rest in peace, my old mucker."

Sara swallowed down the sudden lump that appeared in her throat. "Okay, time's getting on now. If you have nothing further you want to add, we'd better be on our way."

"I can't think of anything. Can I ask how he went?"

"I'm not at liberty to divulge such information, sir. Suffice it to say, the outcome wasn't pretty. You've been most helpful. My condolences on the loss of your friend."

"Thanks. Any idea when his funeral is likely to be held? Will it take place here or back in Denmark? I'd like to pay my respects."

"The best advice I can give you on that one is to leave it a few days and then contact his wife, Mie. Do you know her?"

"I know of her. Obviously, me working long, late hours here, our paths haven't crossed that often. She seemed a nice enough lady. I'll give her a call in a few days."

"She's away in Newcastle, collecting her daughter at present. Bear that in mind when you try and contact her."

"I will. I'll be snowed under with this place for a few days. Look, I'm sorry, I've been as much use as a chocolate fireguard. Do you want to leave me a card in case I hear anything around here that might prove interesting?"

"You read my mind. I was about to suggest the same. Thanks for finding the time to chat with us, we really appreciate it."

"Always keen to help the police. My motto is, I can never know if I'm likely to need you guys in the future. Good luck with your investigation. Hope you find a break in the case soon." He held out his hand for them to shake.

"Thanks, we'll be in touch if we have any further questions. Is that all right?"

"Sure. I have nothing to hide, Inspector."

Sara smiled and, together, she and Carla left the nightclub. "He seemed nice enough. Can't say the same about his establishment. Sounds like a bloody knocking shop to me, a high-class one at that."

Carla sniggered. "You are funny. Is that term even used nowadays?"

"I don't know, is it?"

They both laughed and wandered back up the high street to the solicitor's. Sara sensed they'd be a little early. Hopefully the receptionist would take pity on them and offer them a cuppa.

No such thing. The receptionist insisted they take a seat in the waiting area until their four o'clock appointment came around. *Only fifteen minutes to go. What joy!*

The time dragged, and Sara's anger mounted. Finally, the client slotted in before them left Felix's office. He saw the upset woman to the door and bid her farewell then turned his attention to Sara and Carla.

"Sorry for the delay, Officers. If you'd care to follow me."

The office was decked out in either cherry wood or mahogany. Sara had trouble distinguishing between them.

"Take a seat," Dick Felix instructed.

Sara and Carla settled themselves in the two seats available. "Thank you for seeing us today, Mr Felix."

"No problem. May I ask what this is about? And please, call me Dick or Richard if you prefer."

"Thank you. We've been informed that Lens Jensen is a personal friend of yours, is that correct?"

"Yes, we go back years. May I ask why you wish to know?"

"We're investigating Mr Jensen's murder."

"Are you sure it was him?" He ran a hand over his face and then through his steel-grey hair.

"Yes, sir. It's been confirmed. We're in the process of doing the rounds, speaking to his friends and associates to see if anyone can give us a reason or possible motive for his death. I don't suppose you can guide us in any way?"

He shook his head slowly. "I'm at a loss what to say. I can't believe what I'm hearing. Murdered, by whom? Okay, that was a dumb question. If you knew the answer, you wouldn't be here. Heck, I'm not thinking straight. Why? Who could possibly do such a thing to Lens? He was a decent enough chap."

"That's what we're trying to find out. We've already spoken to your friends, Ray Carmel and Barry Normont. They had a similar reaction to you. Both nonplussed by the notion that someone could kill him. Unfortunately, that doesn't help us going forward. What we need to establish is whether someone had some form of grudge with Lens."

He fell silent for a moment as he thought. "I don't think so, or at least, I can't think of anything off the top of my head. Bugger, I'm in a daze, truth be told. He was a good friend of mine. We shared many a happy time, the four of us, over the odd bottle of wine or a few beers. We put the world to rights, or so we thought—often that wasn't the case. Sorry, I'm chuntering on."

"That's okay. In the circumstances, I'm sure we'll forgive you. So, nothing is coming to mind? Has he fallen out with anyone, sought your professional advice perhaps over the past few months?"

"No, nothing at all. I'd tell you if I could put my finger on anything, but I can't. Damn, was it just him, or was Mie involved in this, too?"

"No, the incident took place not far from his business address. He was found in the river. Mie is aware; she's on her way to Newcastle to inform their daughter in person rather than divulge such sensitive information over the phone."

"Quite right, too. I think I'd do the same. Lizzie was exceptionally close to her father. She's going to be devastated, as will Mie, I'm sure."

"She is. Did they have a happy marriage?"

"Mie and Lens? Yes, as far as I could tell. I can't say I ever heard him say a bad word against her."

Sara raised an eyebrow. "We're aware of his...how shall I put this? Ah yes, his philandering ways. Are you telling me that didn't cause a rift between Lens and his wife?"

"Not that I know of, no. He told me they had an open relationship. Crikey, if my wife ever found out I had a bit on the side she'd take a knife to...well, you get what I'm saying. Maybe it was his culture that allowed him to get away with it."

"So we've been led to believe. It didn't affect your relationship with him in any way?"

"No, why would it? Each to their own. It was nothing to do with me what he got up to. Was it his culture or simply a sign of the times for some? Let's face it, most girls tend to spread their legs at will these days."

"Really? Is that what you truly believe?" Sara asked sternly.

"Sorry if that's caused any offence. You asked for my opinion, that's what I honestly believe."

"Okay, there's two sides to this age-old argument. Bear with me while I point one side out to you. What you're really saying is that it's all right for men to play the field, be surrounded by dozens of beautiful women on a promise, but when a woman sleeps with more than one man, not at the same time, I hasten to add, she's either a whore or a slapper?"

His shoulders slouched. "I'm sorry, I didn't realise what I was saying. People have the freedom to behave as they want without me sticking my bloody oar in. Mind if we start again?"

"Of course. It's easy for people to cast aspersions that could prove to be unfounded. Did Lens ever mention that he'd fallen out with anyone at work?"

"No. He always treated his staff well. They practically ran the haulage firm for him while he..."

"Was out sowing his oats?"

"Exactly. I've tried to think of an occasion where he was annoyed and set on revenge. Most of us go through times like that, right? I can't think of any such thing with Lens. He was a genuine sort of guy. Men and women alike appeared to be drawn to him. Murdered? Who would do such a thing?"

"We intend to find out. We're struggling at present to find any possible motives or clues as to why someone would want to rob Lens of his life. The problem is, without something to cling on to, our investigation will be a lengthy one. It might even mean that it ends up as unsolved."

"Surely not. What about CCTV footage? Isn't that where most leads come from nowadays?"

"You're right. Except there aren't any cameras around the haulage yard." *I'll get the team checking the cameras in the immediate area for Lens' car.*

"I would have thought Lens would have installed cameras on site."

"Maybe; however, the crime itself was committed a fair distance away, close to the river running alongside the premises."

"Ah, I see where the problem lies and the dilemma you find yourselves in, Inspector. I'm really not sure I can add anything further. Yes, we were close friends, but I think in retrospect Lens was also a loner. By that I mean, he mostly kept his private business from the rest of us, apart from the women. That's my take on things. You'll have to ask the other two men what they think, I'm sure they'll back me up."

"Having spoken to them, I fear you might be right. If you can't help us further, then we'll leave you in peace. I'll give you one of my cards. Ring me if anything comes to mind. So far, we have very little to go on and are already chasing our tails."

"I appreciate how difficult this must be for you. Have you been informed when the funeral will take place?"

"No, it's far too early for that to be discussed. Thank you for seeing us." Sara rose from her seat.

Carla flipped her notebook shut and followed Dick Felix and Sara out of the room. He shook their hands at the front door.

"Please, do your best, his family deserves answers, Inspector. We all do."

"Don't worry. The investigation will gain momentum shortly, I'm sure."

On their way back to the car, Sara let out an exasperated sigh. "Okay, we've been at it all day, and what conclusions have we come to?"

They reached the car and got in then continued the conversation as the traffic mounted around them.

"That he liked women more than the average man," Carla said.

Sara nodded and puffed out her cheeks. "Could we be looking at one of his bedmates doing the deed? Perhaps jealous that he'd moved on to a new partner?"

"I guess anything is possible at this stage. All these people have said the same, that the Jensens had an open relationship. I don't profess to know what that entails, nor do I want to know, firsthand, at least," Carla added.

"Okay, let's get back to the station. Maybe the team will have something of value for us, because, as of right now, this case is truly going nowhere fast." She glanced up at the roof of the car and said, "Please, please give us something to go on?" Sara started the engine and eased out into the traffic.

They were about to pull into the station car park when a call went out over the radio. "All available cars to The Dwyer Mansion out on Worcester Road. An explosion has occurred."

"Crap, do you know it?" Sara asked, hurriedly spinning the car around in a three-point turn.

"I think so, vaguely."

"You'll have to give me directions."

7

---

*I*t was chaos at the mansion when they arrived. Several squad cars, two fire engines and an ambulance lined the large drive where the explosion had taken place. Sara nudged Carla and they rushed through the onlooking crowd of emergency staff to where Lorraine was standing next to her van.

"Jesus. You got here early, how come?" Sara asked, her gaze drawn to the charred vehicle as the under-control blaze died down.

"I received the call. I was in between PMs and decided that my team and I needed to get here ASAP."

"Why? You won't be able to get in there until the fire has been put out."

Lorraine grinned. "Call it morbid fascination on my part. These hunks will have it put out in a few minutes. We should be able to assess the scene within half an hour—that's a total guesstimate on my part."

"Is that your fella over there, Carla?" Sara gestured with her head.

Her partner's gaze travelled through the crowd of firefighters tackling the blaze. "Yep."

"What I wouldn't give to see his commanding skills with a hose in my bedroom," Lorraine muttered.

Sara sniggered, but Carla only shook her head in disgust at Lorraine's smutty words.

"She was joking, Carla, lighten up," Sara said.

"How do you two do it? When people are dying, how can you stand there and make dumb jokes?" Carla walked away.

"Ouch, that was uncalled for," Lorraine said, sounding hurt.

"She's worried, that's all. It's a dangerous job."

"Yeah, I appreciate that. Maybe she should reconsider her relationship with Fireman Sam if that's how she feels."

"I'll have a proper chat with her when we're done here. She's right about one thing: we shouldn't be messing about when someone has just died. Shame on us."

"Don't you start. I'm not going to change, Sara, not for her or for anyone else. She doesn't have to cut up dead bodies day in, day out, I do. This is my way of dealing with the harsh realities that death brings."

"I'm sure deep down she realises that. My take is, she's witnessed Gary putting his own life in danger again and it's made her tetchy. Bear with her. Ignore if you have to."

"Don't worry, I'll do that all right."

"Do you know how this happened yet?" Sara asked, peering over her shoulder at the mansion behind them.

"There's a woman in the house. I caught a glimpse of her, youngish, might be the daughter. She put the call in, according to the first copper on the scene. He told me the owner of the vehicle was just setting off somewhere when the car exploded."

"Possible malfunction or a deliberate act?"

Lorraine shrugged. "Until my guys can get in there and get a closer look, your guess is as good as mine."

Sara narrowed her gaze and pushed her for an answer. "You can do better than that. A hunch-guess?"

"Don't quote me on this, but I'm more inclined to think of this as a deliberate act. Of course, at this early stage, I have nothing, nada, zilch, to corroborate that assumption."

"You're pretty smart about these things. I'd rather trust your gut instincts than mine any day of the week. So, are you saying we're only dealing with one corpse here?"

"I believe so."

"That's a blessing. I'll collect Carla, and we'll go and question the woman in the house, see what she has to say. I don't suppose you're privy to the victim's name, are you?"

"A Jack Annibal. I think I've got the surname right."

"It's a start. Thanks. I'll let you know how we get on." Sara headed in the direction of her partner and tapped Carla on the shoulder. "Come on, you, we've got work to do."

"Okay. Do I have to apologise for my outburst?"

Sara shrugged. "If you want to. It's not me who took the brunt of your anger, though, it was Lorraine. We have to walk past her to get to the house, so maybe an apology wouldn't go amiss."

"Okay, you win."

"A word of caution, if you can't stand the heat, get out of the kitchen. And yes, that succinct pun was intended."

"But…" Carla halted first and her head dipped.

Sara stopped a few steps ahead of her and stared at her. "Don't tell me you've fallen for him?"

"I tried not to. I swear I did. He treats me well, Sara. You know what a bonus that is in a relationship."

Sara walked back and hooked her arm through Carla's to get her moving again. "I do. I'm delighted for you, truly I am; however, you're going to have to search for a happy medium. You're bound to see him in action during the working day. If you go to pot every time we meet up…" Sara left the rest of the sentence hanging, hoping her partner would see what she was getting at.

"I hear you. I promise I'll behave."

Lorraine eyed them warily as they approached.

"Sorry, Lorraine. I was wrong to snap at you. Am I forgiven?"

Lorraine punched Carla gently in the arm. "You're forgiven."

Sara pulled on Carla's arm. "Come on, you two will have me in bloody tears soon. We have work to do."

They continued the journey across the deep gravelled path to the front door. They spotted a young woman standing in the bay window in one of the downstairs rooms, staring at the scene.

"She seems bewildered. I hope we get some sense out of her," Carla said.

"You're right. We'll soon see." Sara rang the bell.

The young woman must have sprinted through the house, because within ten seconds the front door swung open.

Sara and Carla showed their warrant cards, and Sara introduced them. "Sorry, your name is?"

"Fiona Merryman."

"Would it be okay if we came in for a chat, Ms Merryman?"

She held open the door, her gaze locked on the scene behind them until Carla closed it once they'd stepped over the threshold.

"Come through. If you're looking for answers, I don't have any. I'm too traumatised to think and put my thoughts into some semblance of order."

Sara put the woman's age at around twenty-two, possibly twenty-three, no more than that. In the hallway, on every available surface, were gold-framed photos of the woman with an older gentleman sporting a greying beard. They appeared to be loved-up in the pictures. Sara's heart jarred with emotion for the woman's loss.

She showed them into a huge bespoke kitchen with a large centre island. The rear wall of the house was made of glass and overlooked a patio area which led to an abundance of shrubs and a magnificent full-sized pool.

Fiona settled into one of the leather couches near the bi-fold doors. She slipped off her shoes and tucked her legs underneath her.

"Maybe you can start by telling us who was in the vehicle and what your relationship with that person was?"

"He was my fiancé." She flashed a huge solitaire engagement ring at them. "Jack Annibal." Tears welled and slid down her cheeks.

"I'm sorry for your loss. While I understand completely how difficult this is for you, the more information we have to go on from the outset, the quicker we'll be able to find out the cause of the explosion."

"I'll tell you what I can. Forgive me if I break down."

"Of course, that goes without saying. Can you tell us where Mr Annibal was going?"

"We were going away to a friend's house in Manchester to celebrate their wedding anniversary with them."

"I see. You say 'we'. You were due to be in the car, too, is that correct?"

"Yes. On the way to the car, I realised I'd left my phone behind. Jack was annoyed. He continued towards the car, he got in, and boom. I was in the hallway by this time. I'd found my phone and was just putting it in my bag when I heard the explosion. I ran to the door and screamed. I scanned the area, praying that he'd escaped, but I couldn't see him. That's when I rang the emergency services. Oh heck, this is unbelievable. He didn't deserve to die like this, no one does."

"Has your fiancé had any problems with the car recently?"

"No, nothing. It's brand new. He only picked it up a few weeks ago. This was the last thing either of us expected to happen. Oh God, a few minutes later, and that could have been the end of both of us." Her hands covered her face, and she openly sobbed for the next few minutes.

Sara and Carla glanced at each other.

"Would you like me to make you a drink?" Carla asked tentatively.

"I need alcohol, for the shock. Can you pour me a tonic? I'd prefer a gin but…"

Carla rose from her chair and wandered around the centre island where she proceeded to open all the cupboards in her search for the alcohol requested.

"You've had a lucky escape. Sorry to have to ask you this, but did your fiancé have any enemies that you're aware of?"

"Off the top of my head, I don't think so. I worked with him. I was his secretary for a while until we got together. I think if he had any enemies, I would have known about them."

"What was his career?"

"He was into letting properties. A property management company. Sorry, my head is all over the place."

"Were the properties owned by him? Is that what you're saying?"

"Yes, that's right. He's been doing it for years. Things have changed in the last few years due to the government's new taxation on second homes or buy-to-let homes."

"And that was affecting the business?"

"Yes, he was in the process of selling off a lot of his properties."

"What about his competitors in the business?"

"That could be anyone. There are people out there on the prowl for the cheapest properties on the market. Jack used to be involved with that side of things, but as I said, he was in the process of selling off some of the properties—not really in the market for buying or adding to his portfolio, I should say. Am I making any sense? I don't know what I'm saying." She peered over her shoulder at the garden and then back at Carla as she accepted the tonic water. "Thank you." She downed half the drink in one gulp.

"If he was selling off properties, what type of people were buying them, can you tell us that?"

"Ordinary people. The prices were too high to attract other investors, way too high."

"What price are we talking about here?"

"Around the three hundred grand mark. Jack mostly bought the properties for around one hundred and forty and let them out to folks as affordable housing. Once a tenant took the mick, he kicked them out, renovated the home to a high standard and flipped it. Sorry, sold it."

"When was the last time a tenant did the dirty on him?"

"About a year ago. Really, it was nothing. Jack employed a security firm to deal with any troublemakers, so nothing came back on him."

Carla whipped out her notebook, anticipating Sara's next question.

Sara asked, "The name of the security firm?"

"Windass and Sons. They're based in Hereford. I could look up the number for you."

"There's no need. We'll find it and make contact with them. Reliable, were they?"

"Totally. Jack has used them for a number of years. It was worth paying out for him to have peace of mind. Jack ran a smooth operation. I really can't point the finger at anyone who would be annoyed with him. Is that what you think? That someone deliberately set out to kill him?"

"No, not really. It could be something like a manufacturer's fault. We're just covering everything from the start. What make of car was it?"

"An Alfa Romeo. They're reliable, so I'm told. I'd rather this go down as a mechanical fault than have the thought of someone deliberately targeting Jack running around in my head. Not sure I could cope with that. God, what if someone did do this and their aim was to kill both of us?" She buried her head in her hands again.

"Please, there's no point thinking like that until the pathologist and her forensic team have done their job."

She dropped her hands and wiped her tears on the sleeve of her thin jacket. "How long is that likely to take? Will I be safe until then?"

"We'll put the house under surveillance. Unless you choose to stay elsewhere for a while, that would be my suggestion."

"Okay, I'll pack a bag and stay with my parents for a few days. Not sure I'd feel comfortable being here by myself right now with all this going on."

"The tech teams will probably be here for the next day or two, trying to figure out how this occurred. It would be better if you weren't around. If you give us a mobile number where we can contact you, that would be great."

She reeled off a number, changing the last digit after making a mistake, and Carla jotted it down.

Sara pressed on with the questions. "Have you been in this house long?"

"No, only for a few months. Jack has owned it for around fifteen years."

"So your relationship was a fairly new one then?"

Her gaze dropped to the shiny, black-tiled floor. "No, it's complicated. Jack was married when our affair began. He finally divorced her about three months ago. I refused to move in until the divorce was finalised."

"I see, and where does Jack's ex-wife live now?"

"Still in Hereford. Over in the King's Acre area. I can find an address for you if you really want me to."

"Thank you, that would be helpful. Private addresses are harder to find than business ones," Sara said, referring to the fact that she had declined the address of the security firm moments earlier.

Fiona left her chair, staggering a little as she stood. "I knew it was wrong of me to sit on my legs."

Sara smiled at her and watched the young woman leave the room.

"She seems nice enough, even if she did have an affair with a married man," Carla whispered.

Fiona entered the room again, a plain red address book in her hand. "Here we go, Michelin Road, number eight."

"Excellent, that's very helpful. Do they have any children?"

"No, Maria was unable to conceive. It put a terrible strain on the marriage. Our affair wasn't intentional. I was there to listen to his woes about how abysmal his married life had become, and things went from there really."

"How has the divorce affected his wife, do you know?"

"She accepted it as far as I know. I've never had much to do with her and I don't think Jack has contacted her since the day of the divorce."

"Was there any animosity between them?"

"Not on Jack's part. He was a kind, considerate man. Yes, we had an affair, and that might paint me as a nasty person, but I can assure you, I'm not. We loved each other deeply."

"I don't doubt that. Does Maria have any family living close by she can call on?"

"No, they're all up in Cheshire, I believe. Jack's family are in the Manchester area. Oh God, I have to bloody ring them. I'm bound to get the blame, aren't I?"

"Why should you?"

"Well, aren't people bound to say that if he'd stayed with Maria this would never have happened?"

"I don't think so. The cause of the incident is yet to be established.

I think you're being too harsh on yourself, especially as you say you and Jack were in love."

She sniffled. "There's something I haven't told you," Fiona said, placing a hand over her stomach.

Sara had an inkling of what the young woman was about to say next. "Go on?"

"We'd just found out that I'm pregnant. Jack was over the moon about the baby, and now...he won't be around to see it, to care for it, to bring it up as his own. That's all he ever wanted in this life, the part that was missing for him. That's why I forgot my phone. Since finding out about the baby, my mind has been all over the place. Oh bugger, how am I going to cope without him? What will the future hold for me and the baby?"

Sara sighed. "That's such a shame. I'm sorry to hear that." She wanted to say so much more but stopped herself. This was a very tragic incident indeed, given all the facts now available.

"Who else knew about the baby?"

"Only our parents. We were about to make an announcement at the gathering we were going to attend. Life can be so unfair, can't it? It's what he always wanted, and now...he'll never hold his own child in his arms. That's what I'm finding the most distressing about all of this. He came so near to having a child of his own only to have his life snatched away from him. How does one even begin to get over something like this? I wish someone would tell me. I'm trying hard not to get upset. I know how dangerous that can be for the baby. I'm going to do all I can to keep this little one safe for the next seven months. I'll be sure to talk to him or her about their daddy every day, tell them what his hopes were for them."

"I'm sure you'll be a wonderful mother. I'm so sorry you're going to have to go through the pregnancy, and all that comes after it, alone. It seems so unfair, especially with what Jack went through to get to this point. If you can't think of anything else, we'd better be making a move."

"I can't. I'm sorry for bogging you down with all my anxious thoughts. Thank you for being patient with me. When am I likely to hear how the accident or incident was caused?"

"I'd say within the next week. Take care of yourself. Here's my card. Ring me day or night if you think of anything or need to speak to me about the case."

Fiona walked slowly as she showed them to the entrance. She eased open the front door, peered out and withdrew quickly. "Oh God, I can't look." Tears tumbled onto her cheeks once more.

"No problem. No one is expecting you to be courageous about this. It's a shocking thing for you to have to deal with. Go back inside, let them carry out the delicate operation. My suggestion would be to go to your parents' as soon as possible. Do you want me to call them for you?"

"No. Thank you for the offer. I'll ring them now, break the news and see if Dad will come and get me."

Sara nodded. She and Carla headed towards the car, their gazes drawn to the emergency crews still hard at work. They took a slight detour to speak to Lorraine.

"Hi, how did it go with the woman? Was it his daughter?" Lorraine asked.

"No, his partner, and she'd just found out she's pregnant."

"Damn, did he know?"

"Yes. She was supposed to be in the car with him, forgot her phone. She went back for it, and *kboom!*"

"Bloody hell, that poor woman. That's not what she told the first officer at the scene, but I'm guessing her mind was all over the place because of the explosion."

"I think we can make allowances on this one. She blamed her pregnancy for the fact that she'd forgotten her phone."

Lorraine nodded, but Sara also noticed the glint in her eye.

Sara shook her head. "You don't think she's behind this, do you?"

Lorraine hitched up a shoulder. "Let's just say, stranger things have happened. Being extra cautious, it might be something that you should delve into. How long had they been together?"

"She's lived here a few months, so she said. Since his divorce came through, although they were having an extra marital affair before that."

Lorraine's eyebrows shot up into her shocking-red fringe. "A divorce, eh?"

"Give me a break. I'm not going to ask any intrusive questions until you can clarify how the explosion occurred. There are so many manufacturing faults with vehicles at present. Let's do our best to rule that out first and then start dig, dig, digging."

Lorraine pulled a face. "Whatever way you want to play it. Aren't you putting yourself under pressure taking this case on when you're in the middle of the Jensen case?"

"I didn't think about that when the call came in. I'll pass it over if the team get snowed under. I think we can manage both cases at the same time; we're quite proficient at our jobs, you know," she added, a note of sarcasm in her tone.

"All right, there's no need to bite my head off."

Sara laughed at Lorraine's defensive retort. "I wasn't aware that I had. Anyway, back to business. How long before you can get in there and start nosing around?"

"My guess is not for a few hours yet. I'll see how it goes. I might head back to the lab and return later."

"That's a bummer. Okay, we're going to shoot off. We'll start the investigation in the morning. Hopefully you'll have a definitive answer for me by then."

"I wouldn't hold my breath if I were you."

"I'll try not to. I'm enjoying my life as it is at the moment. Ring me, no matter what time it is, when you find your conclusive evidence either way."

"You have my word on that."

They made their way back to the car. Carla seemed distracted, and Sara followed her gaze.

"He's excellent at holding his hose in place," she quipped.

Carla tutted and glared at her. "Funny, not. Is it wrong for me to be concerned about him?"

"No, not in the slightest, but all he's doing is putting out a fire. I don't mean to discount your concerns, as they're logical, but if we were attending a fire at a high-rise building, along the lines of *Towering Inferno* then, and only then, would I share your apprehensions. How long did you say he's been a fireman?"

"I don't think I have. Around six years, I believe."

"That's six years of experience he has under his belt. Stop worrying. If you don't, you're going to end up a nervous wreck every time you hear he's attending a scene."

"You're right. Let's get out of here. I've had enough for one day. Tell me we're finishing now?"

Sara glanced at the clock on her mobile: almost seven-thirty. "Yep, let's start afresh in the morning. I'm going to check the team have all gone home for the night before I head home."

"You're forgetting something."

Sara tilted her head. "I am? What's that?"

"You have to drop me back at the station to collect my car."

"Oh right, of course. Let's get cracking then. I have a man to get home to."

"Lucky you. Mine will be tackling blazes all night long."

They slipped into the car and eased through the other emergency vehicles and back onto the quiet main road. Sara bid her partner a good evening and entered the station. She ascended the stairs only to find the incident room in darkness. She almost jumped out of her skin when a finger tapped her on the shoulder. "What the heck?" She turned to find DCI Carol Price standing behind her. "You scared the beejeebers out of me, ma'am."

"Sorry, I spotted you on my way out. Everything all right?"

"Yes and no. We attended an explosion earlier. I dropped Carla back to her car and thought I'd check the team had gone home."

"Ah, I see. What type of explosion?"

"A car. No point asking if it was intentional or an accident, as I don't know yet, not until the forensic report comes in."

"I see. Aren't you already working on a murder case?"

"That's right. I think we'll be able to manage both cases. I'll shout if we need help."

"You do that. Come on, I'll walk out with you. How's that nice young man of yours? And your father, of course?"

"They're both fighting fit, thanks for asking. You're working late tonight. Any specific reason for that?"

"Not really. Thought I'd stick around and clear my desk a little, nothing else for me to do at home."

"Oh dear, do you want me to start playing my violin?"

"No. Sympathy is the last thing I need."

They parted at the main entrance.

"Call on me if you need any advice on your two cases, Inspector."

"I will. Have a good evening, ma'am."

"You, too."

Twenty minutes later, and Sara had arrived home, feeling weary. That quickly dispersed the second she stepped through the front door and spotted Misty running up the hallway to greet her. She scooped her furry friend into her arms and snuggled into her neck. Misty's response was to purr loudly and rub herself under Sara's chin.

"Enough of this, I have a dinner to prepare. I wonder what delights I can find in the freezer for your new daddy and me to eat. You'll be satisfied with a tin of food, as usual. Thank goodness you're easy to please." She kissed the top of Misty's head and placed her gently on the floor.

A quick search through the freezer, and she came up trumps with a chicken curry she'd prepared a few weeks earlier. After defrosting it for ten minutes in the microwave, she placed the curry in a pot. In another saucepan, she put a couple of servings of brown rice which she covered with boiling water and lit the gas below them both. Then she ran upstairs to the bedroom and stripped off her work clothes, replacing them with a leisure suit she preferred to lounge around in at home.

Hearing the key in the door and Mark calling out her name, she ran down the stairs and straight into his arms.

"Wow, what a welcome. What's this in aid of?"

She touched his face. "Some days are crappier than others, and when I come home to the best partner in the world, it makes life worth living, that's all."

He kissed her gently on the lips. "That's lovely to hear. I've missed you. I was tempted to ring you during the day between patients, but I figured you'd be up to your neck in the new investigation. How's it going? Wait, don't answer that, let's eat first, I'm starving. Can I help prepare the dinner?"

"Nope, it's all in hand. Chicken curry is on the menu."

"Fabulous. Does this mean we get to try out that new chutney we bought from our trip to the Hop Pocket?"

She took his hand and led him into the kitchen. "Glad you reminded me, I'd forgotten all about that. Any idea where it is?"

"I've tucked it away safely at the back of the cupboard."

She laughed. "It's there to be eaten, idiot."

"Only on special occasions, and homemade chicken curry is definitely one of those."

Sara slapped his arm. "Cheeky sod. Don't think I missed the damning inference there."

His mouth dropped open then quickly slammed shut again. "Honestly, I never meant anything by that. I'll lay the table, do something useful other than putting my foot in my mouth."

"I should."

Sara dished up the meal which went down a treat. Together, they cleared up the kitchen and then opened a bottle of wine and retired to the lounge to watch a movie.

At eleven, they let Misty out to do her business and then secured the house for the night and retired to bed.

Around twelve-thirty, Sara woke with a start and realised her mobile was ringing. She switched on the bedside light and answered the call, presuming it would be from Lorraine, cursing herself that she'd told the pathologist to ring her ASAP with the results of the tests. She was wrong.

"It's me. Sorry to wake you," Carla said, sniffling.

Sara sat upright and prepared herself for bad news. Mark stirred in the bed beside her, and she reached out for his hand and held it tight.

"Oh God, is it your dad?" he whispered.

Sara shook her head and mouthed, "It's Carla."

He sat up and rested his head against hers to comfort her.

Sara placed the phone between them to let him hear the conversation. "What is it, Carla?"

"It's Gary. He's been in an accident."

"Is it serious?"

"I think so. I've received a call from his commanding officer, asking me to go to the hospital. I'm scared, Sara, I don't know what to do. I know that sounds foolish…"

"Not at all. Do you want me to come with you?"

"No. Sorry, I didn't mean it that way. What if I go there and find him at death's door? How will I cope?" Carla sobbed.

Sara's heart hurt for her friend and partner. "You'll cope, Carla. You're resilient, made of strong stuff. I'll willingly come with you, if that's what you want."

"I don't. I'm sorry I called you. I'm confused. Goodnight, Sara."

"No, don't hang up. I'm here for you. It doesn't matter what time of the day or night you need me, I'm always here."

"Thank you." Carla sniffled. Then she hung up.

Sara sighed heavily. "Damn, did you get the gist of that?"

"I did. We should go, she needs you. I'll come with you."

"I can't go against her wishes like that, she'd never forgive me. Maybe I could ring the hospital, see if they can tell me what's wrong with him."

"I doubt it, you're not his next of kin."

"No, but I'm a DI in the police," she barked. "Sorry." She leaned over and kissed him.

"You're anxious, that's understandable. I don't mind going to the hospital with you."

"Let me try and ring her back, see what she says." She dialled Carla's mobile number.

"Hi, I'm on my way over to the hospital now. I'll deal with the consequences when I get there. Sorry I woke you."

"Don't be. We're friends as well as partners. I would've been upset if you hadn't rung me. Let me know what you find out when you get there. Did his commanding officer tell you how the incident occurred?"

"Not really. He's going to be there at the hospital and will explain when he sees me. It must be bad if he's been hospitalised. I'm scared, Sara."

"I know. You'll be fine. Remember, he's in the best place possible. Ring me as soon as you know. Thinking of you both."

"Thanks, you're a good friend, Sara Ramsey."

"Take care, drive safely."

"I will. Speak soon."

Mark threw back the quilt and walked out of the bedroom. He returned a few minutes later with two steaming cups of strong coffee. "Here you go."

"You're a mind-reader. Thanks for this. I'm still tempted to go down there. I wouldn't want to step on her toes, though."

"Why don't you leave it for a few hours? Hopefully Carla will ring back with some news soon."

"It's the waiting I hate. I won't be able to sleep now."

"You will, eventually. There's nothing you can do. No amount of stressing will help the situation either."

"I know you're right. I'll go downstairs, let you rest."

He pecked her on the cheek. "If that's what you want. Call me if you need me."

Sara slipped on her towelling robe and collected the quilt off the spare bed and settled down on the sofa. She watched the time drag by all night and finally plucked up the courage to ring Carla at six the next morning.

"It's me. How are things?"

"Oh, Sara. It's worse than I feared. Gary was crushed between two vehicles. They're not sure if he's broken his back or not. They're preparing to send him down for an MRI scan now."

"Oh heck. Hang in there. I'll come to the hospital and sit with you."

"No, there's no point both of us being here. You get some rest. I'll call you as soon as I have any further news. I can't see me making it into work today."

"Don't even consider showing up today. I'll make Price aware of the situation. I'm so sorry you're both going through this tough time."

"I dread to think what lies ahead of us if he has broken his back. How will we cope?"

"You will, I have no doubts about that, love. Ring me when you can."

"Thanks, I will."

Sara closed her eyes and drifted off to sleep for the next hour. Mark woke her with a cup of coffee.

"Any news?" He sat on the quilt by her feet.

"Suspected broken back."

He ran a hand through his hair. "Shit! I hope they're wrong. That's likely to be a life sentence for the pair of them."

"Don't say that. Damn, why does life have to be so shitty?" The tears she'd fought hard to hold back slipped down her cheeks.

Mark gathered her in his arms. "We'll be there to support them."

She drew back from him and smiled. "You're a special man, Mark."

"You're pretty darn special, too, Ms Ramsey."

8

*S*ara drove into work on autopilot that morning, arriving before the traffic had a chance to entrap her. She spent the first hour attending to her paperwork as she waited for the rest of the team to show up. Once they were all seated at their desks, she drew their attention and shared the devastating news.

The room fell silent until Jill said, "Poor Carla. Is there anything we can do, boss?"

"At present, all we can do is pray that Gary is going to pull through this and that the doctor's initial diagnosis is wrong."

"I'll get a collection started, if that's all right?" Jill replied.

"Let's leave that a few days, Jill. Carla will know we're all thinking of her. Let's see what the prognosis is first. Right, I don't mean to sound cold-hearted, but we have work to do. Two urgent cases to solve, one a murder enquiry, and the other, well, I'm not too sure what we're dealing with yet, which reminds me, I need to chase up the pathologist, see what she can tell me." She went on to tell them about the explosion and what she'd gleaned from the preliminary interviews so far. "How are things looking on the Jensen case?"

"We haven't discovered much at all, boss." Will shrugged, a down-hearted expression on his face.

"Keep your chin up. It's only a matter of time before some clue comes our way. Carla and I spoke to three of Jensen's friends yesterday. All of them mentioned his philandering ways. My suspicion is that possibly one of his former bedmates likely killed him when he moved on to pastures new. Proving that is going to be incredibly difficult when no one is supplying us with the names of his conquests." Sara heaved out a sigh. "I think I'm going to have to rely on the media to help us out there. I'll chase up the Press Office bods and arrange a conference to take place today, in the hope that some of these women will come forward. It's a tricky one; I don't really want the wife to know what we've found out yet, not while she and her daughter are grieving." Sara was reminded of the remnants of the party she and Carla had witnessed at Mie's house the day after her husband's murder, still pondering if that type of thing was a tradition to the Danish. "So, we have a lot to be getting on with and we're one woman down. I've cleared my desk for the day; therefore, I can lend a hand with any background checks that need doing on both cases."

"Would it be worth looking at the CCTV footage for the second incident, boss?" Craig asked, raising his hand like he usually did.

"Yes, why not? The victim owned a mansion. I'll get the address for you."

"It's all right, boss, I have it here."

"Good. First job for me is to ring the pathologist. I'll be right back, hopefully with some worthwhile news to get us started."

"Do you want us all working on both cases, boss?" Barry asked.

"At the moment, yes, until things become clearer, and then we'll go from there. Does anyone fancy filling Carla's shoes for the day and tagging along with me? Don't all rush to volunteer," she added, grinning as she scanned the team.

Craig tentatively raised a hand. "Would you mind if I did it, boss? I'm dying to get out in the field."

"I hope you're speaking figuratively there, Craig. Okay, if no one else has any objections, then consider yourself promoted to my partner for the day or for the foreseeable future."

The red tinge colouring his cheeks told her how embarrassed he was, and she wondered if it was only just dawning on him what he was letting himself in for.

"Thank you, boss. Does this mean I get to call you Sara?"

The others either chuckled or gasped.

Sara hid the urge to laugh and conjured up an angry expression. "You do that, and I'll drop you off in Worcester and tell you to walk home."

"Oh, I see," he stammered.

"Everyone else laughed, and Sara finally cracked her face. "I'm joking. Okay, now you've made me feel guilty for making you all laugh. As you were, folks. Craig, give me thirty minutes. If I'm not out of my office by then, you have my permission to come in and drag me out."

"Yes, boss. I'll try and source the CCTV footage close to the victim's mansion while I wait for you."

"Good." She returned to her office and closed the door behind her, unsure how she felt about Craig riding alongside her for the day instead of Carla. Setting that notion aside for a second, she sat in her chair and placed the call to the Press Officer to organise the conference for either later that morning or the afternoon. "Hi, Jane, it's DI Ramsey. How's it going?"

"Ha! I've been expecting your call. All going well, or should I say it was until you rang. Don't tell me you need a conference organised ASAP?"

"Yay, you know me so well. Is it possible?"

"I'm sure I can wangle it somehow. Leave it with me, and I'll get back to you."

"I have to pop out to interview someone soon. I was hoping to get a rough idea from you before I leave. Any chance?"

Jane tutted and sighed. "I'll need at least ten minutes."

"You've got it. You're a treasure."

"Yeah, you'll bury me one day with your demanding nature, I know that for sure."

Sara chuckled. "I know I ask a lot of you sometimes but I really do appreciate it."

"I know you do. I'll get back to you in a few minutes. Hang tight."

Sara ended the call, sat back in her chair and glanced at the fast-moving clouds as her thoughts turned to Carla and Gary, waiting on the news of his X-ray or MRI scan, whichever the hospital would use to verify a broken back. She wasn't medically proficient in the slightest. She was still in a daze when the phone rang.

"DI Ramsey."

"It's Jane. You're all set for twelve noon. How did I do?"

"You're amazing. I'll be sure to put you at the top of my Christmas card list this year."

"Hmm…I can tell you're lying, you know. I'll be there to hold your hand."

"See you then." Sara ended the call and shot out of her chair and into the incident room. "Craig, get your jacket."

He was in the middle of writing something down, and his pen flew in the air when she called out his name. "Yes, ma'am, um, I mean, boss. I'm good to go."

They raced down the stairs and out to the car.

Once the car was in motion, Sara explained, "Okay, sorry to scare you back there. We need to visit the ex-wife of Jack Annibal to question her, then I have the press conference to attend at noon."

"Will you have enough time to prepare for it?"

"No, I'll wing it like I usually do." She turned to face him and laughed. "Don't look so shocked. Most officers in my position do the same thing. The case is all in our heads anyway, so it's not as if we're taking the piss or anything."

His gaping mouth closed again. "Glad to hear it. I have to say, watching you closely, not in a stalkerish kind of way, I'm amazed at what you achieve in a working day."

"Ah, sucking up to the boss time. Are you guilty of something? If so, now's the time to tell me."

"No, me? Never! I wouldn't know where to begin. Oh damn, I'm all tongue-tied now. Sorry, there's me trying to be professional and I'm blethering like an idiot."

She laughed. "I have that effect on people. Just chill. A word of advice: let me do all the talking. I hope your note-taking skills are up to scratch."

"They are, boss. I'm so excited you chose me."

She laughed again. "It's not as if I had an option. Let's be fair, you were the only one to volunteer, not that I'm the type to take offence."

They arrived at Maria Annibal's address a few moments later. It was a detached property on the edge of the city, on a small new-build estate.

"Notebook at the ready, and make sure your pen is in working order before we enter the house, Craig."

He scribbled on the back page of the book. "All in order. Am I allowed to be a tad nervous?"

"Of course. You wouldn't be human if you weren't. I'll let you in on a secret: I'm always a little nervous on such occasions, too."

"You are?" he asked, surprised.

Sara smiled and pressed the doorbell.

A busty redhead opened the door with a frown etched into her forehead. "Hello. If you're selling something, I'll pass, thank you. Buying this place last month has wiped me out." She started to close the door.

Sara held up her warrant card and introduced herself and Craig. "Would it be okay if we came in for a chat with you?"

"May I ask why?"

"I'd rather say inside."

"If you must. Come in." She allowed them to enter and pointed at the first door on the right off the hallway. "The lounge is in there. I have a cat. I hope you're not allergic. If you are, I'll put her out."

"I'm not, I have a cat myself. Constable, are you?"

"Not as far as I know. Not had much to do with them in the past."

With the pleasantries out of the way, the three of them took a seat in the snug front room. Sara reflected on how this house was a stark contrast to the mansion where Maria had lived previously and couldn't help wondering if the woman could have any possible grievances about that.

"Now, what's this about? I have an appointment at the hospital at eleven. I hope you're not going to take up too much of my time."

Sara's hackles went up immediately. "We'll try not to. I'm not sure if you've been informed or not...I'm guessing you haven't. Yesterday afternoon, at around five o'clock, I attended an incident at your former address."

Her frown deepened. "I'm not with you. Which address?"

"The mansion you shared with your ex-husband."

"Ah, I'm with you now. Had an argument, have they? Knew it would only be a matter of time."

"Who are you referring to?"

"Jack and his bit of skirt. The one he dumped me for. Not that I'm bitter. I'm better off without him. Twenty odd years of marriage, and this is what I have to show for it." Her hand swept around the room.

"Are you sure you're not bitter? You sound very upset to me."

"It's called anger. It presents itself only when his name crops up. Other than that, I've accepted the situation and got on with my life."

"Okay. Well, unfortunately, the incident I had to attend was that of an explosion."

Maria's eyes grew as wide as footballs. "An explosion? The house exploded? Is that what you're telling me? Some form of gas leak, was it?"

"Not the house, no. Your former husband's car exploded."

Maria's hand flew up to cover her mouth, and she gasped. Dropping her hand into her lap moments later, she whispered, "No. Was anyone injured?"

Sara nodded. "Sadly, your ex-husband was in the vehicle when the explosion occurred. There was no way for him to escape it."

Maria rocked back and forth in the armchair. "No, please, don't tell me that. Don't tell me Jack is dead!"

"I'm afraid he is. Shocking, I know."

The tears flowed. "Oh no, I can't believe what I'm hearing. I know I hated that man at the end because of what he and that bitch did to me, but this...damn, his mother will be so distraught when she hears the news."

"As would anyone, I suspect. I know how upsetting this is for you;

however, I wonder if you wouldn't mind answering a few questions for us."

"Questions? About the explosion?"

"Not necessarily. The truth is, I've spoken to Fiona, and she has drawn a blank as to who would want to hurt your ex-husband—"

"Wait, you're telling me this wasn't an accident? I just assumed it was."

Sara held her hand up. "At present, we're unsure if this is related to a manufacturing fault or if it really was a deliberate act. We won't know the outcome of the forensic results for at least forty-eight hours. In the meantime, I suppose I'm being extra vigilant trying to seek out any possible motives someone might have for carrying out the incident on purpose."

"What? And you thought you'd show up at my door?"

"Please, don't get angry. I'm not here to accuse you of anything. I'm simply here to search for answers or possible clues. Would you be willing to work with me on this?"

Maria inhaled and exhaled a few deep breaths and wiped her eyes with a tissue she plucked from a box on the side table beside her. "I'll do what I can, of course I will. It would be callous of me not to."

"Thank you. Before you divorced your husband, did he ever receive any type of threat?"

Maria thought over the question for a second or two. "No, I don't think so."

"What about former employees, any animosity there perhaps?"

"Not that I know of. He rarely sacked people. Usually slept with the female employees— well, one of them comes to mind, that slapper, Fiona."

"Would you mind answering a few questions about that or would it be too raw for you at this time?"

"Fire away."

"I take it you were upset when you learnt the truth?"

"Of course, wouldn't you be?"

"I dare say I would, yes. When did you find out?"

"Around six months ago. My whole world collapsed when he

blurted it out over dinner one night. I hit the roof, slung my plate at him; he managed to duck just in time. My aim has never been that sharp, regrettably."

"You're saying that you would have caused him damage if you could?"

"Yes, but it was the anger speaking. I would have regretted my actions if I'd managed to hurt him." Her gaze dropped to the carpet. "I'm sorry he's now dead. He didn't deserve that. No one deserves their lives to be ended so cruelly."

"I agree. Again, I must reiterate, we're unsure if this was an accident or not."

"I understand. I've thought and thought and can't come up with a possible name for you. He was a likeable chap, really. He had his flaws that finally destroyed our marriage, but what man doesn't? Sorry, that came out wrong. I meant him having flaws. All men have them, right?"

"I suppose so, as do women. None of us are perfect, as much as we like to think we are."

"True. See, I really don't know what I'm saying and proving that I'm no use to you at all. This news has affected my way of thinking."

"Understandable. So, are you telling me that during your twenty-year marriage, Jack never fell out with anyone?"

"I can't say that for definite. We all fall out with people occasionally. We wouldn't be human if we didn't. I truly don't think I can tell you more. Why don't you speak to Fiona? Maybe she has a jealous ex-boyfriend looking for revenge?"

"Possibly. I didn't question her much because of her condition." Sara winced when Maria frowned. *I forgot she doesn't know about the baby, damn!*

"Condition? What con...no, you're not telling me she's *pregnant?*"

"Sorry, I shouldn't have mentioned it. We'd better get on. I'm sorry if I've stirred up feelings which you had stored away. I hope you understand and forgive the nature of our visit."

"I do. I'm sorry I can't help you further. I'll show you out." Maria shook her head and seemed shocked by the unwelcome news.

The three of them left the lounge.

Sara dug a card out of her jacket pocket. "Ring me if you think of anything relevant in the coming days. I appreciate you seeing us today. Sorry that it was to share such bad news."

"Thank you. I will. I hope you find out this was just a tragic accident, soon. Goodbye."

She closed the door gently, and Sara and Craig returned to the car and headed back to the station.

~

*M*aria watched the detectives drive away from her bedroom window, then she picked up her mobile.

"Mie, it's Maria."

"Hi, how are things going?"

"How could you do that? How could you? I thought we agreed not to go through with that method."

"We did? I don't recall that being the outcome of our conversation. 'Do what you have to do' were your exact words. Hey, don't blame me. Once the ball is rolling on something like that, it's far too difficult to back out. He's a professional. I'm taking it he did a good job then?"

"If you're asking if he successfully killed Jack, then yes, he did. I'm devastated by this. Plus, I've had the police here asking all sorts of questions that I simply couldn't answer."

"Like what? Bloody hell, I hope you didn't drop me in it."

"Of course I damn well didn't. All I'm saying is that you should've warned me when 'the hit' was going to take place."

"What would be the fun in that?" Mie laughed.

Maria's anger rose. "You're twisted. I wish I'd never got involved in this idiotic murder pact. You wait until I tell the others. I bet they'll have second thoughts about it as well."

"Don't be ridiculous. You're overreacting. For fuck's sake, you killed my *husband*. All I'm guilty of doing is getting someone else to kill your pathetic ex. It's a shame *she* wasn't in the car as well when it blew up. Two birds and all that."

"The police just told me that Fiona is pregnant. You're sick. I thought I knew you, but evidently I don't. I want nothing further to do with this agreement."

"I'm sorry to hear about the pregnancy, but in my eyes it changes nothing. The others won't thank you for backing out now. So she was having a baby, so what? I don't see what your problem is…oh shit! It's more than that, isn't it? Don't tell me you were still in love with him?"

Maria closed her eyes. She'd never spoken to the other girls about how deep her feelings ran for her ex-husband. She'd tried her hardest to hate him for how he'd treated her but failed. She had been with the same man, the only man she'd ever slept with, since her teens. It was hard, so hard to discount those feelings as incidental and worthless.

"Maria? Answer me—no, forget that, it's obvious you still love him. Why didn't you tell us?"

"Didn't you love Lens?"

"No, I fell out of love with him years ago. Why would I love a philandering shit like him? I'm sorry, sweetie. You're grieving. Look, I should be back by around seven. Why don't we meet up later? Come over to my place, and I'll cook for you."

"I can't."

"Why? Because you'll be wallowing in self-pity?"

"Don't start on me, Mie. Have some compassion for once in your damn life. Oh God, forget I said that. The last thing I want to do is fall out with a former terrorist."

"Jesus Christ. Now you're being downright stupid. So, I have a few old connections that come in handy now and again."

"Now and again?" Maria asked, gobsmacked.

"Don't take everything so literally, Maria. This was a one-off, I swear to you."

"Forgive me if I don't believe you. I can sense the lies are tumbling out of your mouth right now. Damn and fuck, why did I ever sign up for this? It all started out as a joke amongst friends. You were the one who was dying for someone else to kill Lens off, weren't you? Because you were too damn scared to do it yourself. Just like Jack, you haven't fucking dirtied your hands there either, have you?"

"Get off your high horse, love. You're not so perfect. You must've been riddled with anger over the divorce, otherwise, why would you even contemplate killing off another woman's husband, namely mine? Don't paint yourself whiter than white, it won't wash with me, I'm warning you."

Maria was seething by this point. "I wish I'd never laid eyes on you. I've always seen something dangerous in you. I should've known better than to call you a friend."

"Whatever. My hands are far cleaner than yours are right now. I'd be careful what else you say during this conversation."

"I don't have anything left to say to you. Maybe your hands are clean because when it came to the crunch, your nerves couldn't hack it."

"Maybe that's true. Ring me when you've calmed down. Or call one of the others if you need to chat about this further."

"Maybe I'll ring that inspector instead and reveal the truth behind our husbands' deaths."

Mie said, "You really don't understand the magnitude of what we've done, do you? If you go running off to tell tales, you're only going to incriminate yourself and you'll likely spend the rest of your life behind bars. Is that truly what you want?"

Maria chewed her bottom lip and remained silent. Without saying anything further, she hung up.

She had a lot of thinking to do. Some of it was going to be exceptionally difficult to handle.

9

*S*ara phoned Lorraine on the way back to the station. "Any news about the explosion yet?"

"I was plucking up the courage to ring you."

"Shit, now you're scaring me. What was it?"

Lorraine's breaths came in short, deep bursts. "After careful consideration and a lot of discussion and research by my team…"

"For God's sake, it's like waiting for paint to dry. Get on with it, woman."

"Impatient cow. My team believe it was an expertly built device reminiscent to something that might have been used by the IRA to cause so many atrocities back in the eighties."

Sara yanked the car over. A driver blasted his horn as he passed her car. "This isn't one of your shitty wind-ups, is it?"

"I'm actually offended you should think that."

"Shit! I'm sorry. How the heck does something like this happen after all these years? Crap, I need to get back to the station and look into this. See if the victim had any connections in Ireland. Bloody hell!" Sara slammed her clenched fist against the steering wheel half a dozen times until the pain worked its way into her wrist and lower arm.

"We'll do some digging at this end, see if anything shows up in our system to help with a connection. This could always be a one-off."

"The likelihood of that is?"

"Don't ask. I know it's a shock, but you need to get over it—and quickly."

"I'm over it already. One last thing before we get on. I'm a woman down. Carla is at the hospital with her young man. He had an accident while on duty last night, suspected broken back. I thought you should know. We're going to be under pressure on this one."

"Fecking hell. A broken back? Jeez, let's hope the docs are wrong about that. Send her my love and tell her I'm thinking of them both when you next speak to her."

"I will. I'll be in touch soon." Sara turned to face Craig. "Did you get the gist of that? Sorry, I should have put it on speakerphone. I was too stunned to think straight."

"I did. You think the IRA are behind this or could we be looking at a copycat?"

"Your guess is as good as mine on this one. Mind-blowing either way. The question is, do I tell Fiona or not?"

"What about the press conference? Are you going to reveal the truth then?"

"I haven't figured that out yet. I'd like to cover both deaths during that but I'm cautious about muddying the water when it comes to putting the information out there. It could be confusing for the general public. Oh God, I don't know. This news has bloody astounded me. I think I'm going to run it past DCI Price." She indicated and pulled out into a gap in the traffic en route to the station. "Yes, that's what I'll do, pass the buck on this one, see what she suggests. My mind is swimming."

"It is unbelievable. Never thought we'd have to combat these types of crimes on our shores again," Craig admitted.

Sara's mind whirred, and she drew into her parking space at the station after conducting the rest of the journey on autopilot.

"Do me a favour and bring the team up to date for me while I see Price."

They bolted up the stairs and separated at the top. Sara barged into DCI Price's outer office, startling Mary who was engrossed in her work.

"Hello, Inspector. Is everything all right?"

"Not really. I need to speak with DCI Price urgently. Is she available?"

"I'll ask." Mary left her desk, tapped on the door to her right and entered. "Excuse me, DCI Price. DI Ramsey would like an urgent word with you if you can spare the time."

"Show her in, Mary."

Mary smiled and stepped aside. Sara flew past her and babbled until she ran out of breath.

"Whoa, back up a little. A bomb, and you suspect the IRA are responsible?"

Sara nodded and sucked in another anxious breath. "Yes, that's what it amounts to. We could be dealing with a copycat, there's no telling at this stage. Jesus! No. I don't want to be dealing with this crap full stop, and yes, that's purely because of selfish reasons. I think Mark and I have been through enough shit to last us a lifetime. If I start investigating a crime involving the fucking IRA, that's going to put both of our lives in permanent danger."

"Sit down and calm down. We don't know the facts. Let's not get ahead of ourselves here."

"The facts are that a bomb was attached to a car and it exploded, here, in Hereford, on my damn turf." She tugged a clump of her hair at the roots.

"I said calm down. I appreciate why you're getting yourself into such a state, Sara, but that's not going to solve anything, you hear me?" Carol Price left her chair and walked over to the table on the far side of the room and returned with a glass of water. "Here, drink this."

"I will if you put some bloody alcohol in it."

"Not on my watch, lady. Okay, where do we go from here?" Carol asked, retaking her seat and tucking herself under the desk again.

"I was hoping you'd guide me on that one, boss, hence the visit.

I'm at a loss where to start. Carla's not around so I can't bounce ideas off her."

"First things first, how are things with Carla?"

"I haven't heard. I'll ring her this afternoon. She should know something definite about Gary's condition by then."

"Okay. Let's hope for good news for them both there. Right, I'm going to have to inform the super about this. My suggestion would be to prioritise the bomb case. Can you leave a member of your team dealing with the original investigation and throw the rest of your resources to solving the second one?"

"If I have to," Sara replied, her reluctance prominent in her tone.

"I understand your hesitancy to get involved in this one, Sara, but what it comes down to is that you're the best investigating officer we have. If you don't take the case, we're fucked. Excuse my bluntness, but that's a fact. I understand your reluctance is for personal reasons. I'm also asking you to put that aside for now."

"You're asking me to put two people's lives in jeopardy, more than that if you include the rest of my family as well. The IRA notoriously went after relatives of the police officers. I can't put my family through that, boss."

Carol's gaze fell onto the paperwork on her desk and remained there for several moments while she thought. "I understand. However, you swore to protect and serve when you signed a contract with us."

Sara's mouth gaped open. Seconds later, she replied, "I can't believe you're pulling that one on me. Are you telling me that if I refuse to investigate the case, I'll lose my job?"

Carol closed her eyes and clenched her fists. Opening her eyes again, she said, "If I have to. Don't let it come to that, Sara, please."

Sara left her chair, the chief's gaze on her as she walked back to the door. "I'll think about it. I have a conference to prepare for."

"Don't mention the IRA during the conference. We need to ensure the higher-ups are privy to this information before we start sharing it with the public, got that?"

"Loud and clear, boss. Loud and clear." Sara left the office, smiled tautly at Mary and marched, heavy-footed, back to the incident room.

The team all turned to face her.

She perched on the nearest desk and sighed. "Someone get me a coffee, will you? I need to organise what's going on in my brain before I share what I've been told."

Craig tipped his chair back in his haste to get to the vending machine. He returned with a hot white coffee with one sugar, and Sara took it gratefully.

"Thanks, I appreciate it." She took several sips of the boiling drink, blowing at it in between. "Okay, here's where we stand. The DCI has instructed us to prioritise the Annibal case because of the obvious possible connections with the IRA. However, I'd like at least one of you to remain on the Jensen case. Any volunteers?"

Jill Smalling raised her hand. "Would you mind if I stayed on the Jensen case, boss? It's just that I've been doing a hell of a lot of background searches and think I may have uncovered something that I'm finding rather perplexing."

"Sounds intriguing. Okay, you stick with that one. I'll come and see you after we've worked out how we're going to proceed with the Annibal case. Does anyone have any suggestions? My mind is still on how I'm going to play the conference. Bloody hell, what a mess. Why does our job never run smoothly? Don't give me your theories on that one, it was rhetorical. The best we can hope for is that something shows up in Annibal's past. Dig deep, people. I want every route covered, from finances to camera footage around the mansion. Craig, organise house-to-house enquiries—let's keep those within the team for now, okay? God, I hope this doesn't get out in the press, it would cause bloody mayhem." She gulped down half her coffee which was cooler now and went to see how Jill was getting on. She dragged a chair next to the efficient sergeant. "Okay, hit me with it."

Jill searched through the paperwork on one side of her desk and took out a sheet which she placed in front of Sara.

"What am I looking at?" She glanced up at Jill then back at the writing on the sheet.

"I've been searching social media and come up with a surprising connection. It might turn out to be nothing, but I think it would be wrong for me not to mention it."

"And?" Sara asked, urging the woman to reveal all, aware of the impending conference around the corner.

"Searching through the friends, I've found out that Maria Annibal and Mie Jensen were Facebook pals."

"Interesting. Let's not get too carried away with that just yet. It could be a coincidence. After all, they both live in Hereford."

"Okay. Do you want me to keep digging?"

"Definitely. See if their husbands knew each other, either through Facebook, or perhaps they were business associates or have been over the years. Let's not cast this aside, not yet."

"I'll get digging. Good luck with the conference."

"I'm regretting calling it. What the heck am I going to say? For the first time in ages, I don't have a bloody clue."

Jill glanced at her, her expression full of sympathy. "You're an expert at these, you'll figure it out."

"I wish I had your confidence. My mind is all over the place. Will you remind me to ring Carla upon my return?"

"Of course."

"Thanks. Right, I'm off to do battle with the journos." She drained the rest of her drink, collected a notebook from her office and made her way downstairs where she met up with Jane Donaldson.

They entered the conference room together to face the awaiting reporters.

*A*t the end of the conference, which consisted of Sara mainly skirting around the main issue and dodging all the relevant questions the frustrated journalists were asking, she left the room and went back upstairs.

She needed a break. Jill caught her attention, making the sign for her to call Carla. Sara smiled her appreciation for the reminder. She bought two coffees from the machine, handed one to Craig to repay him for the one he'd bought her earlier and settled herself behind her desk.

She rang Carla's mobile number. "Hi, it's me."

"Hi." Carla sounded dead on her feet.

"I didn't ring first thing in case you hadn't heard any news. How's Gary?"

"They told me a few minutes ago that the prognosis is better than they anticipated. Don't ask me to repeat all the medical jargon they used. The main thing is, his back isn't broken."

Sara tilted her head and blew out a relieved breath. "Oh God, that's excellent news."

"He still has a long road ahead of him. He's a determined bugger. I doubt his injuries will keep him down for long."

"I'm sure you're right. Did they say how long they're expecting him to stay in hospital?"

"It depends. They'll have to wait for the swelling to go down first, and there's still a risk of internal bleeding, so they need to watch out for that. It's such a relief to see him conscious and alert."

"I'm glad to hear it, Carla. Will he be up for a visitor this evening?"

"Honestly, I think it's best if we stick to family members for now. Even I'm feeling like an intruder being here."

"Why? You have every right to be there. Don't let anyone bully you into thinking otherwise."

"I didn't say they were. Why do you always have to jump to conclusions? It's a personal thing. We haven't been going out together that long and…"

"Okay, I can understand that. Sorry for shooting my mouth off. How are you holding up? You sound tired."

"I haven't slept a wink since I got here. Once he's more settled, I'll think about going home. I'm getting the impression that his mum would rather be caring for him herself. That's not to say she's been nasty to me. She hasn't done or said anything disparaging, I'm just picking up on the vibes."

"Then let her do it. All mothers would react the same in these instances. Take the opportunity to get some rest yourself, love."

"In other words, get back to work, I need you."

Sara noted there was no laughter attached to her partner's words. "Not at all. Take your time, we'll still be here, ready to welcome you back with open arms."

"Thanks. I was going to see how the rest of the day goes and come back tomorrow, if you'll have me."

"Leave it another day. Use tomorrow to catch up on your sleep. I've got to get on. Send Gary my best wishes. And most of all, take care of yourself. Ring me if things get too much and you need to vent or want to chat."

"I will. You're a good friend, Sara. Good luck with the investigation."

"Thanks. Take care, Carla." Sara hung up. She'd deliberately not spoken to Carla about work. She had enough on her plate, and Sara was worrying enough for both of them anyway.

The rest of the afternoon she spent surrounded by her team. Barry and Will had left the office and were conducting the house-to-house enquiries at the properties closest to Annibal's address. Sara was anxiously awaiting their report. Nothing so far, and time was marching on; it was almost five o'clock.

The conference had aired on the radio during the afternoon and was about to feature on the local evening news at teatime. Again, disappointingly, the phones remained silent, free from useful and the usually dud information, which generally filled their notebooks when an incident of this nature occurred, not that they dealt with many explosions in Hereford.

Sara checked to see how Jill was progressing with the social media angle around five-thirty. "Anything else?"

"Not really. I called Jensen's friends and work colleagues, the ones you'd already spoken to, and none of them could place Jack Annibal."

"Interesting. Okay, let's leave it for now. Go home, get some rest, and we'll probe things further in the morning. I know we wanted to avoid asking the wives how they know each other, but I think, going on the blanks you've drawn so far, that we might need to do that. I'll consider it overnight. Yet another unsuccessful day at the office, eh?"

"Yeah, I hear you. What makes matters worse is we're talking about two cases having the same frustrating elements to them, not only one."

"Exactly. Let's hope something positive comes our way soon. With the notion that the IRA might be involved, the added pressure on this case could have a detrimental effect on our careers. Let me correct that: on *my* career. Hell's bells, all we bloody do every day is come to work to do our jobs, and this nightmare lands in our laps."

"I'm sure once we find enough clues it'll all piece together quickly." Jill held her crossed fingers in the air.

"I ruddy well hope so. Okay, everyone, let's call it a day. See you bright and early. Thanks for all your hard work today."

10

*M*ie stomped around the house, livid because of the call she'd received from Maria. She urged herself to calm down. To take what her friend had told her with a pinch of salt. However, the more she tried, the more irate she became.

It wasn't until she spoke to a few of the others that her anxiety levels decreased. She needed a good time. That was her, after all. She'd always been known as a professional good-time girl, throwing the odd swanky bash now and again. She didn't have time to lay on one of those but she did have time to organise a small soirée for her dear friends, the others in the pact. Everyone except Maria. She wasn't welcome enough to set foot in her house again any time soon, not until she stopped sulking over something that had already taken place and was out of her control.

Lizzie had remained in Newcastle as she had a few exams she needed to attend in the next few days. She'd been distraught by the loss of her father but had assured her mother she wouldn't let him down by failing her exams. She admired her daughter's strength, unsure whether she'd have been able to push aside her grief if her own father had died when she'd been at university. She was relieved Lizzie hadn't come home with her. She would have struggled with the added pressure.

After dressing the table with the stunning tapas she'd spent the last few hours throwing together, Mie had a quick shower and dressed in an elegant marine-blue evening gown and welcomed the first of her friends to arrive.

"Jacqueline, how are you?"

They kissed each other continental style, four times on the cheek, the same way they had greeted each other for nigh on ten years. Mie was relieved to find at least one of her friends was still able to treat her the same way.

"I'm wonderful. Glad you called me. Things were getting a little fraught at home."

"Is Alan up to his old tricks again? Treating you like a second-rate object? I bet you can't wait for Di to do the deed, can you?"

Jacqueline's gaze dropped, and she ran a finger around the rim of her champagne glass. Mie recognised the signs, and her heart sank. *Not another indecisive mare?* She placed her glass on the bar in the lounge.

Her friend quickly changed the subject. "You look glamorous tonight. I feel like a tramp, a well-dressed one, but nothing compared to you." Jacqueline glanced down at her beige trousers and sparkly black top.

Mie linked arms with her and picked up her glass again. "Nonsense, you look as sophisticated and as charming as ever. Ignore me, I felt like dressing up. I didn't mean to make you all feel awkward. Imagine me in my PJs if it will make you feel better."

"Can't wait to meet up with the others. I hope Maria is all right. I saw a press conference on the news tonight about an explosion at Jack's mansion. You'll have to give us the gory details later."

"Sore point. Maria isn't coming. We fell out earlier. Rather than go over how the conversation went, I'll wait until we're all here, if that's all right. I get bored repeating myself."

Jacqueline placed a slender hand on her flushed cheek. "Oh heck. Okay, I'll wait. I hope you two can patch things up. It'd be a shame to fall out over something…"

"So trivial?"

"Not quite the word I was searching for in the circumstances…"

Jacqueline was interrupted by the doorbell ringing a second time. Mie excused herself and answered it. Di stood on the doorstep, dressed in jeans and a dark jumper.

"Bugger, you could have warned me this was one of your swankier dos, darling. I'll nip home and get changed. Start without me." Di turned away, but Mie caught her arm and dragged her into the house.

"Oh no you don't. So? I went over the top. I'm allowed. Bloody hell, this week has been so damn liberating. I can't tell you what a relief it is to do what I want, when I want, without Lens criticising me for letting my hair down—not that he was around much in the evenings. Come through to the lounge, Jacqueline is already here."

"Good, I'm glad she's here. This is why I've dressed down. I've decided tonight is the night."

Mie gasped. "Really? You're going to bump Alan off this evening? You'll have to tell us how you're intending to do that."

They entered the room to find Jacqueline sneakily tucking into the food.

"Caught you nicely." Di rushed forward and kissed her on the cheek four times. "You'll get fat."

"Nope, I have a high metabolism. Even if I do put on a few pounds, I'll go on a ten-K run to get it off. Wow, you really know how to make an effort for one of Mie's fancy shindigs, don't you?"

"Don't you start. I have an excuse, I promise. Not sure you'll want to know about it, though."

Jacqueline tilted her head as Di accepted a glass of champagne from Mie. "Go on, enlighten me."

"I've arranged to meet Alan later to do the deed."

Mie and Di both glanced at Jacqueline to gauge her reaction.

"Oh heck. Fuck. Goddamit, why the shitting hell did you go and tell me that for?"

"Sorry. Bloody hell. Do you need to sit down? You look paler than a virgin's knickers, girl."

Jacqueline staggered over to the couch. Mie stared at Di and shrugged. They both joined her on the couch.

Mie sat on the arm closest to her friend to avoid creasing her beautiful gown. "Are you all right, love?"

"I'm not sure how I feel. Bugger, I'm stunned. Christ, if I feel like this now, what state am I going to be in when you've kil...after he's gone?"

"Do you want me to postpone it, is that what you're saying, Jackie?" Di asked, placing a hand over Jacqueline's.

She snatched her hand away and shook her head. "I don't know. Why? Why do I feel this way when I hate the man so much?"

"Human nature. You'll get over it. Look at me, I couldn't be happier."

Jacqueline glanced up at Mie. "You're different to me."

Mie stood, affronted. "Meaning what?" she snapped back.

Di stood between them. "Ladies, let's not let this get out of hand. We had a pact, remember that. Two of us have already completed their end of the bargain. That leaves two of us to complete our tasks. I'm going to proceed with meeting Alan tonight, Jackie. Get over it."

"*Get over it*? Get over *what*? That you're about to murder my husband?" Tears bulged in Jacqueline's eyes.

Mie reached for a tissue and handed it to her emotional friend. She sighed. "Jacqueline, if you want to pull out of the deal, well, it's a bit late for that. I wasn't going to tell you this, but here goes. Maria isn't coming tonight, not because she is attending another function. I told you both a fib. No, she rang me earlier to reprimand me for killing Jack the way I chose to kill him."

"She did? What are you saying? That you two have fallen out over this damn pact?" Jacqueline demanded.

"I suppose so. She'll come around. I'll give her the space she needs to come to terms with Jack's death. Okay, wait, during the conversation I sensed that she was still in love with him, despite their divorce. She admitted she was; however, she also told me that the police had been round her house today to question her, indirectly, of course. They wanted to know if she knew anyone with a motive for killing him. Then they told her that Fiona, you know, the bit of skirt he installed in the mansion once he'd kicked Maria out, well, she's pregnant."

Jacqueline covered her head with her hands and groaned. "Fucking hell. How did this happen? A stupid pact that is tearing us all apart."

Mie grabbed Jacqueline by the shoulders and pulled her to her feet. The two women stood with their noses almost touching. "It is not tearing us apart. Once Alan is out of the way, think of the freedom you'll have. Take my word for it, you'll never look back, I promise you."

"That's bollocks. I don't think I can do this. Yes, Alan has been a proverbial pain in the arse with all his affairs…well, I've been thinking about that and I instructed a solicitor to start divorce proceedings today."

"You've done *what?*" Mie shouted, tightening her grip on Jacqueline's shoulders until her fingers dug into her flesh.

"Ouch, you're hurting me. Let go of me, Mie."

Seething, Mie let go and marched to the other side of the room to glance out of the French window, aware that if she didn't calm down she was likely to slap Jacqueline for being such an imbecile.

Di spoke, trying to be the peacemaker between the three of them. "I agree with Mie; you shouldn't have done that, Jackie, but then, what's done is done. I haven't told you this before, but needs must. Alan has been ringing me for years, pestering me for a date. I didn't tell you because I wanted to protect you. He's the lowest of the low."

"I don't believe you. You're making this all up, conspiring against me to make me feel bad for wanting to back out," Jacqueline shouted, her hands sitting on both of her slim hips.

Mie turned to face her. "She's not. Di told me in confidence about Alan a few years back. Let her finish him off tonight and be done with it, Jackie. You'll be better off without the cheating bastard. In the long run, we're all going to be better off without our other halves. None of them treat us right, show us the love we deserve, care for us in the right way. You can't deny that, can you?"

Jacqueline gulped. "No, he doesn't care about me, that's why I've sought the advice of my solicitor."

"It's too late for you to back out now, Jackie. The wheels are already in motion, and I'm due to meet him in an hour."

Jacqueline fell silent. Mie insisted that everyone should shake hands and tuck into the food she'd spent the last few hours preparing.

It wasn't long before the three of them were reminiscing about the exciting, action-packed holidays they'd shared every year since they got together and their imminent month away on a Caribbean island.

The fraught tension eased until it was time for Di to leave. "Are you sure about this, Jacqueline?"

The two women had plied Jacqueline with several glasses of champagne without her realising it over the past hour or so.

She raised her glass and said, "To Di's successful encounter and the demise of my cheating son of a bitch husband. I'm so ready to live my life again. To freedom!"

Mie and Di chinked their glasses against Jacqueline's and shouted, "To freedom."

Moments later, Di pricked up her ear at the sound of a horn beeping in the drive. "That's my taxi, girls. Wish me luck." She hugged Mie first and then turned her attention to Jacqueline who was by now swaying with the effects of the alcohol. "Good luck. Knock 'em dead," she slurred.

Mie and Di chuckled as Mie showed her friend to the front door.

"She'll be fine once the reality hits," Mie said.

Di shook her head. "I'm not so sure. I'm in two minds whether to call the whole thing off."

Mie smiled and opened the front door. She gently shoved her friend over the doorstep. "Go. Don't think about it, just do it. Good luck, my dearest friend, your turn is just around the corner. Think about that when you're finishing him off."

"I hope to Christ this doesn't jeopardise our friendship. I'll ring you later, let you know how it all went."

"I'll be up until the early hours of the morning, no doubt. I'll ensure Jacqueline is tucked up in bed by the time witching hour descends upon us."

Di waved and hopped in the back of the taxi. Mie watched the car leave the drive and then returned to her tipsy guest in the lounge, only to find Jacqueline asleep on the couch with three fluffy cushions under her head for comfort.

Mie kissed her fingertips and placed them on Jacqueline's cheek. "Sleep well, lovely lady. All your problems will be solved soon."

~

*T*he cab driver dropped Di off at her luxury four-bed home, ten minutes later. She rushed up to her bedroom to get changed. The dress she had chosen to wear was a slinky red calf-length number that had a huge split up the right thigh which left very little to the imagination. Once she'd applied her makeup, she checked everything was as it should be in the en suite bathroom. It was. All the items she needed were to hand. She brushed her hair, trailing it sexily over her shoulder. The doorbell rang, which set her heart racing. *No chance of you backing out now, girl!* She studied herself in the mirror and hoped all the effort would be worth it. *Worth it? What am I saying?* With what Alan had in mind, she doubted he'd be concerned with what she was wearing.

Di summoned up her best smile and opened the door, leaning seductively against the edge as she welcomed him. He reached for her hand, and she pulled him close. They shared a kiss that sent her pulse rate off the chart. *Wow, who'd have thunk it? I've always thought his kisses would be something akin to latching on to a trout.* She closed the door behind him.

"I've waited so many years for your call. What made you change your mind?" he whispered between the kisses he was planting on her neck.

"I don't know. Does it matter? You're here at last. We're here, together."

"We are. One question: where's your hubby?"

"You don't have to worry about him. He's out of town for the night on business."

"Okay, that's great. What do you have planned for this evening?

You look sensational, by the way." He took a step back and admired her slim figure with curves in all the right places.

"I'll leave that to your imagination." She took his hand and led him up the wide staircase to the bedroom. Releasing his sweaty palm, she sauntered across the room and sat on the end of the bed, crossing one leg over the other, ensuring her long, shapely pins were on show. Patting the bed beside her, she smiled. "Aren't you going to join me?"

In his haste to get to her, he almost tripped over the shoes that he was trying to lever off his large feet. She suppressed a snigger.

He bounced up and down on the bed. "Very comfy. It would be even more satisfying if we were between the sheets, naked."

"I have something much more appealing planned. Why don't you strip off your clothes? I need to use the bathroom. I'll join you in a moment."

He didn't need telling twice. He'd torn his jacket and shirt off, showing his slender, bare chest by the time the bathroom door closed. Again, an unexpected feeling stirred within her. She stared at her reflection and pointed a finger. "Remember the pact. Don't you dare…"

She blocked out the anger reflected in her eyes and opened the bag she'd placed on the toilet. Taking the rope from the bag, she slung it around her neck then opened the door to find a naked Alan on the bed, his head resting on one arm. He was lying on his side, waiting for her to join him. He was exceedingly pleased to see her, judging by the size of his erection. She swallowed back the emotion threatening to emerge and sexily made her way towards him, emphasising the sway of her hips in the process, the swishing sound of the silky material the only noise in the room.

"Why are you still dressed, and what's the rope for?" He wiggled his eyebrows.

The idea had come to her when she had sourced a new bed. This one would be ideal for what she had in mind. "Guess," she replied, running her tongue across her lips. *Bloody hell, what is wrong with me? Has it really been that long since a naked man tried to seduce me?*

Yes, it bloody has. Victor doesn't have a clue about the art of seduction. Not with me anyway.

"Why the hesitation?" he prompted, interrupting her thoughts. He patted the bed next to him.

"No reason, just taking in the wonderful view. You're a big boy. I didn't realise how big until now. I suppose I should have guessed by the size of your feet. My mother always warned me about getting involved with men with huge feet."

He roared with laughter. "She did? Well, it took you long enough to succumb to my advances. I don't have to tell you how important this evening is for me, do I? One thing I need to say first: this is between you and me, right? Jacqueline can never find out about this, ever."

"Oh gosh, of course. Do you think I'm crazy? If she ever found out, well, she'd bloody murder me."

They laughed. "Both of us more like. Now, come here, I've had enough talking. I need some action now, baby."

She removed the rope from her neck. There were four lengths of it. He changed positions, anticipating what she was about to do.

"Hands first," she said, fluttering her eyelashes.

"Whatever you want to do is fine by me, baby."

That's the second time he's used the name 'baby'. Annoying little shit!

He was compliant when she took his right hand in her own and placed it above his head. She tied it securely around the thick wooden post at the end of the headboard and then moved on to tie his other hand. After that, she moved down the bed, stopping to gaze at his giant erection he was intent on waving around. She continued on her journey and tied his feet to the posts at the bottom and jumped off to look down at him. He was now in a star shape with a ten-inch spike at his centre.

It had been easier than she had predicted. How gullible could men be when a night of lustful sex was on the table?

"Okay, now what?" His voice came out breathless and full of desire.

Guilt knotted her stomach. She pushed it aside; she had a job to do.

She dipped back into the bathroom and carried the large bag into the room.

He raised his head to try to see what was going on. "A bag of goodies, eh? Why don't you take off your dress, let me see what you're hiding beneath it? My imagination has been running wild for years."

"Patience, dear man. I need to get everything in place first. Are you ready to have some fun?"

His head bounced up and down as if it were spring-loaded. He was successfully ticking her off with his dumb actions. She found the time to ponder how Jacqueline had put up with the sick shit for so many years. No wonder she was in the process of seeking a divorce. What she had planned for him would save her friend the expense of going through the court system.

"Yeah, baby, yeah. I'm all for having a little fun in the bedroom."

Who does he think he is, Austin Powers? "You say that as though Jacqueline doesn't enjoy sex."

"Oh, she does, when it suits her. She's not that adventurous, though, sadly."

"Is that why you seek your pleasure elsewhere?"

His eyes widened, and his expression was one of shock.

"Don't be shy, answer me. Tell me what your sexual fantasies entail. Maybe we can act out some of those this evening."

"Well, I've always fancied a threesome."

"Boring!" she shouted, louder than anticipated. He'd successfully pissed her off. She reached into the bag and withdrew a large knife.

"What the fu…what's that for?" His gaze went from the knife to his erection and back to the knife. "You wouldn't?"

"Don't tempt me." She laughed. "Don't panic, it's not what you think. I had you worried then, admit it?"

He let out the breath he'd been holding in. "You did. What's it for?"

"All in good time." She bent down to the bag again and this time extracted a funnel.

"Hey, what are you intending to do with that? I've never used one of those in the bedroom before."

"You'll find out soon, I promise," she replied, her tone light and singsongy. One hand holding the funnel and the other the knife, she leaned over him. "Open your mouth, nice and wide."

"What? Why? I need to know what your intentions are first."

She backed away and placed the objects back in the bag. "If you don't want to play along, it's your loss. I'll untie you and let you go back to your boring wife."

"No, wait. I'm willing to give anything a go. You've convinced me."

She smiled and returned to the bag, took out the funnel and the knife and then stood alongside the bed once more. "Open your mouth."

"And if I don't?" he asked playfully.

"Then I'll use this to slice off your nipple."

He laughed. She took the opportunity to ram the funnel in his mouth. He gagged on it and tried to push it out with his tongue.

"Don't struggle, you'll only make things worse. Be a good boy, and the rewards will be mind-blowing, I promise you."

He stopped fidgeting, and his eyes widened as he watched her every move. She dipped into the bag again and this time extracted a small petrol canister. He couldn't see this because she kept her movements low at ground level. She unscrewed the top, her gaze fixed on his. Then she stood and quickly poured the contents down the funnel before he had a chance to register what the heck was going on. She held the funnel in place. He coughed and spluttered, the liquid spilling down the sides of his mouth. She forced the funnel further into his throat. He thrashed around like a shark caught on the end of a hook. She watched with a morbid fascination as the last embers of light in his eyes were extinguished. His eyes were now bloodshot and her bed soiled where he'd shat himself.

"Great job, lady. Now look at the crap you have to clean up." But that was the least of her troubles.

Her plans hadn't included how she was going to get rid of the body and clean up the mess. She picked up the phone and rang Maria.

"Maria, you have to help me."

"Sorry, who is this?"

"Don't be such a bitch. You know damn well who it is. Get over to my house immediately."

"No, I won't be bullied into doing anything else. I want nothing more to do with this pact. What have you done?"

"I've killed Alan. I need your help to dispose of the body. Please, help me."

Maria did the unthinkable and hung up on her. Furious, Di redialled the number only to hear the engaged signal. *Damn, she's left it off the hook. Bloody woman!*

With only one option left open to her, she rang Mie. "Hi, I need your help."

"Why, what do you need, Di?"

"Alan is dead. I need to get rid of his body and clean this place up before hubby gets home tomorrow."

"Shit! Why didn't you think about disposing the body?"

"Don't ask dumb questions. Are you going to help me or not? Maria has already refused to help. I'm desperate here."

"Christ, of course I'll help. I'd never let you down. Give me twenty minutes, I'll have to call a cab—wait, make it half an hour. I'll have to get changed as well and put Jackie to bed."

"Sod it, get a move on." Di ended the call and stared at Alan on the bed, already regretting her actions. *Fuck! It seemed a good idea at the time, and now...* "I'm sorry, Alan, you didn't deserve to die this way." Tears trickled down her cheeks, and she ripped off the sultry dress she had worn to seduce him, tearing it to shreds as anger fuelled her movements and thoughts.

She dressed quickly all in black and waited in the hallway, pacing the area until Mie showed up almost forty minutes later.

Mie paid the taxi driver and entered the house.

Di collapsed into her arms. "It was awful. You have to help me get rid of him. Whatever was I thinking? I utterly despise myself."

"Don't be silly. That will die down. Think of the way he's treated Jacqueline over the years. That should be here," Mie prodded Di's forehead, "at the front of your mind. He deserved it, love, they all did."

"Did they? I'm not so sure."

"You're having doubts about Victor? After the way he's treated you? Not only has he flaunted women under your nose but he's also guilty of hitting you. Out of all of us, you have more right than the rest of us to have a happy existence. Don't back out now."

Di nodded continuously as her friend's words sank in. "You're right. I'm sorry for melting down like this. Come on, we'd better get rid of him."

Di led the way up the stairs.

Mie gasped the second she stepped into the bedroom. "Crap, what did you do?"

"I chucked petrol down his throat."

"Oh my God, I'll have to give you a ten for originality, but bloody hell, Di, your bedroom smells like a damn petrol station. I doubt you're ever going to get rid of the stench."

"Shit. You have to help me; we need to think up an excuse."

Mie opened Di's wardrobe doors. "Find me a pair of jeans you no longer use."

"What? Why?"

"We haven't got time for twenty questions, just do it."

Di searched the bottom of the wardrobe and extracted a pair of denim jeans that had seen better days. "Here, I never use them now, they're tatty and full of holes."

"You're nuts. They'd be highly fashionable to some of the youngsters today. They'll do. Get me the can of petrol."

"There's nothing left. I used it all."

"The whole can? Fuck, no wonder he's dead."

"Don't heap more guilt on my shoulders. I'm struggling as it is."

"It doesn't matter. There must be a few drops left in there. Pour it over the trousers and leave them in the corner of the room."

"Why?"

"You can tell Victor that you filled up with petrol and poured some down your trousers by mistake. That'll do the trick."

"You're a genius. What would I do without you for guidance?"

"Pass. Right, you do that while I untie his arms and legs."

Di did as she was told and returned to help Mie who appeared stressed when she couldn't untie one of the knots.

Di reached into the bag and pulled out the knife. "Here, I'll do it with this."

"Bloody hell, you didn't think to mention you had a knife up here before?"

"Sorry. My mind isn't functioning properly right now."

"You don't say. Right, have you got an old sheet lying around? A dust sheet for decorating perhaps?"

"I think so, it's in the garage."

"Get it."

"But it'll be full of cobwebs."

"It'll be full of a dead body in a moment, woman."

Di didn't hang around to argue. She raced down the stairs, unhooked her garage keys and flew out of the back door to the garage. She found the sheet, shook it out in the garden and then locked the door and ran back up the stairs, two at a time. "Here you go, it wasn't as bad as I thought."

Mie rolled her eyes and snatched the cloth out of her hand. She spread it out on the bed, close to Alan's body, and rolled him onto it. "Don't just stand there, help me."

Di dithered and then got her act together and helped encase the body in the sheet. "What now?"

"Now, we carry him downstairs and out into your car."

"Shit, why didn't you say that? I could have got the car out while I was down there."

"Doh! How else are we supposed to get rid of the body? Seriously, you guys are the pits in the brain department. No wonder I have to do all your thinking for you most of the time."

Di stood back, folded her arms and tapped her foot. "That's grossly unfair."

"Is it? Give me a break and help me move the body. We're running out of time if you want to tidy this place up."

Di grabbed the end where his feet were, leaving Mie to struggle down the stairs with the heavier end.

"Jeez, thanks a lot."

"Sorry, you're stronger than me."

Mie seemed annoyed but got on with the task at hand without making any further comments. They paused a few times en route to take a breather and finally made it to the bottom of the stairs without encountering any major hurdles.

"Get the car out," Mie ordered.

Di picked up her keys and ran out of the front door, pulling it to behind her. She revved the engine and drew up as close to the front door as possible, then reentered the house.

She switched off the outside light just in case any of her close neighbours saw them. After bundling the body in the boot of the car, they hopped in and drove.

"Where are we going?" Di asked.

"Just drive, I'll tell you which way to go."

Twenty-five minutes later, they were out on the A4103 Worcester Road near Bishop's Frome.

"Surely this is far enough," Di complained.

Mie nodded. "Okay, pull over at the next available farm gate."

"You're dumping him on a farm?"

"In a field, yes. Stop arguing and do it."

"I wasn't aware that I was arguing with you. Calm down."

Di searched the darkening hedgerows ahead and almost gave up because it was impossible to see a gap in the moonlight, when a metal gate caught her eye.

Mie must have spotted it at the same time because she pointed and shouted, "Stop! Here will do."

Di pulled the car onto the small strip of grass beside the gate. "Damn, it's locked."

"We'll just have to throw the body over the gate then. Improvisation, that's what's needed here if we want to get home before bloody midnight. I need my bed, girl."

"But he's heavy."

Mie tutted, threw her a pair of latex gloves and slung open the passenger door. Di met her at the boot of the car. Together they lifted Alan's body out and struggled to the gate.

Mie prodded the corpse underneath with her knee to get some leverage. "Okay, let's try and get at least half of him on top of the gate. Hurry, before a flipping car comes along."

They managed to balance Alan's top half on the upper rung of the metal gate.

"Tip him over," Mie ordered.

Alan landed in the field with a thud. Mie climbed the gate.

"What the hell are you doing?" Di demanded, shocked.

"We can't leave him here where everyone can see him, numpty. Quick, hop over and give me a hand."

Di clambered up the gate and jumped down the other side. They moved the corpse a few feet, far enough for the hedge to shield it from the busy road.

"Let's get out of here, pronto." Mie ran back to the gate and swiftly climbed it.

As Di landed on the other side, a lorry came hurtling past and tooted his horn at them.

"Shit! That's all we frigging need. Let's hope the smutty thoughts he was thinking distracted him from taking down your plate number."

"Bloody hell. Did you have to say that? I'm going to be crapping myself now."

"Nothing new there then. The deed is done. We need to get out of here, and for Christ's sake, act naturally over the next few days. Don't bring any attention to yourself."

"I'll try not to. Thanks for your help this evening. I was in panic mode until you came up with a solution."

"That's what friends are for. Next time you kill someone, my advice would be to plan everything out thoroughly."

"*What*? Are you insane? I have no intention of going through this again."

"It was a joke. I promise you, none of us will ever have to go through something like this in the future. Three down, one left to go.

Speaking of which, I'd better get back to Jacqueline and break the news."

"Crap! Rather you than me. Will you go into detail? I'm not sure she'll be able to take it."

"No, I'll skirt around that when she asks." Mie patted Di on the back. "In spite of everything that has happened tonight, you did good, girl."

"I feel terrible. Who would have thought our friendship would come to us breaking the law like this?"

"Let's go. Things will seem a whole lot clearer for everyone once the final murder has been committed. I may sound a little warped when I say this, but I have to say that I've enjoyed it."

"No! Enough for it to become a regular thing?"

Mie shrugged. "Why not? We could set up a business. How to bump off your cheating bastard of a husband."

Di gaped at her.

"For fuck's sake, woman. I'm joking. Take me home."

11

———

*S*ara received the call from the station around six-thirty that morning. She groaned and rolled out of bed and jumped in the shower. When she got out, Mark entered the bedroom with a tray. Two mugs of coffee and four slices of toast and butter.

"You're incredible, thank you so much." She kissed him and grabbed a slice of toast which she continued to nibble on as she dried her shoulder-length hair.

Dressed ready for action and her belly full for a change after receiving an early morning call, she hugged and kissed Mark goodbye and got on the road. She took the shortcut through the back lanes to the location the woman on control had given her and arrived between fifteen and twenty minutes later.

Lorraine's distinctive red hair stood out in the crowd. Several police officers were organising an unnecessary cordon. There wasn't likely to be any gawping pedestrians this far out in the country.

She tapped a constable on the shoulder. "Who told you to do this?"

"Sorry, ma'am, I thought it would be a good idea."

Sara shook her head slowly. "It'll be a waste of time. How many officers do we have here?" She scanned the area quickly and noted at least six uniforms standing around.

"Six of us, ma'am."

"Make better use of yourselves. This road will be getting busy soon. Get it down to one lane. Get some temporary lights working. Make sure they're positioned away from the scene; half a mile that way would be better."

"Good idea. Thanks, ma'am. I'll get that organised now."

"I want two uniformed officers to remain here. Send the rest back to the station, they'll only get in SOCO's way."

"Yes, ma'am."

Sara issued a taut smile and crossed the grassy bank to where Lorraine was instructing her team.

Once her pathologist friend had finished, she turned to face Sara. "Glad you got rid of the excess."

"A tad overenthusiastic for the station to send all of them out here for a dead body. What are we dealing with?"

"I'll get you a suit and show you." She took a few paces to the van and emerged from the back with a white paper suit.

Sara slipped it on, and together they walked through the gate.

"Apparently, the farmer was out here early, tending to his sheep and discovered the corpse lying there, tucked up against the hedge."

"Wrapped in a sheet?"

"Yep, my guys have finished taking all the photos they need for now. I've asked them to erect a tent. Looks like a downpour is on its way."

Sara peered up at the darkening clouds. "I fear you're right. Obvious statement coming up: it looks like the body was dumped here. Over the gate or was the gate unlocked?"

"You've got it. The farmer told me he always keeps the gate locked. Poor man is distressed. He's over there if you want a word, sitting in his tractor."

"Did he see anyone?"

"Nope. Waste of time talking to him if you ask me. He's as much in the dark as we are."

"I'll have a brief chat and send him on his way while you finish getting set up. I'll be right back."

"Good luck. Be gentle with him."

Sara pulled a face at her friend and shook her head at the unnecessary comment. Sara was always tactful in such circumstances. She approached the tractor. The farmer, resting his head on his arms across the steering wheel, neglected to see her coming. She knocked on the door and scared the life out of him. "Sorry. I didn't mean to startle you. I'm DI Sara Ramsey, sir, and you are?"

"Paul Frank. I own this field and the ones surrounding it. I was resting my eyes."

Sara smiled. "No problem. I'm sorry for the inconvenience caused to you at the moment, but I have to ask if you saw anything. Were you out in this field yesterday?"

"I was here, and no, that thing wasn't here then. I rang the police as soon as I spotted what it was. Never had anything like this happen in all the years I've been farming. That's nearly forty years, by the way. Shocking that someone should dump a body in my field. I apologise, that came across as selfish. Of course, I'm sorry that whoever is wrapped up in that sheet has lost their life. Oh, damn, ignore me. I'm struggling to put my words in order."

"Don't worry, I quite understand. Have you possibly noticed anyone suspicious hanging around in say the past week or so?"

"No, no one at all. Which was why this was a complete shock to me this morning."

"The SOCO team will be here for the next day or so. They'll try not to hold you up. I'll give you my card should you think of anything that might help the case. Apart from that, you're free to continue. Thank you for placing the call."

"Okay, I apologise I couldn't be more help. I don't tend to come down this way much during the day. First thing in the morning to feed the sheep, and that's it. No telling how long the body has been there since this time yesterday morning."

"That's helpful. Thanks again." Sara smiled and turned back towards the crime scene.

The tractor started up and set off behind her. She felt sorry for the farmer. Knowing that a dead body having been dumped on his land would probably give him nightmares for months.

"Any good?" Lorraine asked.

"He said he usually comes down to this field first thing in the morning; there was nothing here yesterday."

"Which gives us a twenty-four-hour timeline unless the corpse can tell us otherwise."

They watched the two SOCO team members erect the tent within a matter of minutes. They carried the body a few feet and then placed the tent over it.

"Time to find out," Sara said.

"How's Carla's young fireman?"

"So-so. The good news is they discovered his back wasn't broken, that's a major plus. She's due back to work tomorrow."

"That's brilliant. I bet her mind won't be on the job."

"I think she's professional enough to set her personal life aside for nine to ten hours until her shift has ended."

"Not everyone is as adept at doing that as you are, my dear friend."

Sara shrugged and motioned for Lorraine to enter the tent ahead of her. She followed her in and stood to one side while Lorraine and a member of her team unwrapped the body which had been tied up with a towing rope.

It wasn't long before the sheet fell open to reveal the naked body of a man in his mid-to-late forties.

Lorraine lowered herself to the man's mouth and heaved. "Jesus."

"What is it?"

"Petrol."

"No. In his mouth?"

"With no other wounds on him, I'd say that was the cause of death. Someone forced him to drink petrol then dumped his body."

"Holy crap! Are you sure?"

"That's my initial assessment, Sara. I won't know what the actual COD is until I open him up."

"Bloody hell. I can smell it now. What a horrible death."

"It wouldn't have been a pleasant way to go. I suppose we have to be thankful they didn't put a flame to his mouth."

Sara closed her eyes, trying to shut out the vile image. "Too bloody right. What's the point in using petrol? The two usually go hand in hand—douse someone and set them alight, correct?"

"You've got it. Not sure, could be a number of reasons. Maybe their conscience struck and prevented them from going through with their sickening actions. Could be that they were disturbed—highly unlikely because of the way the body was wrapped up and dumped here."

"Shit, either way, he's naked and without ID. That's gonna be a tough nut to crack."

"I'll do the usual in such cases, run his prints through the database. I'll let you know ASAP what it comes back with."

"That's great. Anything else for me at this stage?"

Lorraine shook her head. "Nothing more."

"I'm going to head off then. I have two other cases I need to get a handle on before any information starts coming in regarding this one."

"Go. I'll ring you if and when I have anything for you."

Sara smiled, nodded and left the tent. She stripped off her suit and left it at the rear of Lorraine's car and returned to her own vehicle. She glanced down the road to see the makeshift lights had just arrived and the remaining two uniformed officers at the scene were speaking to the contractors, passing on Sara's instructions. She drove past them, beeped her horn and raised a thumb.

She arrived at the station in dire need of another coffee. The time was approaching nine, and Sara was lost in thought as she entered the main entrance. She almost jumped out of her skin when someone coughed close behind her. She spun round to find Carla standing there. The poor girl looked dead on her feet. "No way. Go home, Carla. I mean this in a kind and caring way, but you look like frigging shit."

"I'll be fine. Please, I can't sit at home worrying."

"Then go and sit with Gary at the hospital."

Her chin dipped onto her chest. "His mum doesn't want me there. I walked away rather than kick up a stink."

Sara hugged her. "I'm sorry, Carla. It's hard for all of you. I'm sure she didn't mean anything nasty."

Carla stepped back out of her arms. "As far as I'm concerned, Gary and I are over." She stormed past Sara, ran up the stairs and into the ladies' toilet.

Sara rushed to keep up with her. *Damn! What can I say? I haven't got a clue what Gary's mother has said to her to cause this much pain.* Cautiously, she opened the toilet door and stuck her head in. "Is it safe to come in or are you going to bite my head off?"

Carla was standing, propped up against the sink, blowing her nose on toilet paper. Sara stood in front of her.

"I'm sorry. Maybe you should leave me alone for a few minutes."

"What? Until the snot runs dry you mean?"

"You're gross," Carla replied, the briefest of smiles touching her lips.

"I know, but you love me in spite of that."

"Luckily, yes I do. I'm sorry for breaking down like this. I'm an emotional wreck, haven't had a wink of sleep all night."

Sara spun her around to look at herself in the mirror. "I can frigging see that. It didn't take my detective skills long to figure that one out."

Carla returned to her position and wiped her eyes. "Damn, the one day I forget to put my mascara in my bag, I choose to have a damn meltdown at work."

"You can use mine if you need to. Tell me what happened, Carla."

"I was sitting by his bed, I'd been there all day, holding his hand and talking to him, when his mother burst in and told me that she wanted to spend some quality time with her son. She ranted at me that I had hogged enough of his time and now it was her turn to care for him properly, alone."

"Was Gary awake to hear this?"

"Yes, of course he was. Rather than cause any unpleasantness, I left."

"What? And he didn't stick up for you?"

"No. Never said a damn word. I'm not going to get into an argument with someone's mother if they haven't got the balls to speak up when she's in the wrong."

"It's a toughie, getting involved in a mother-son relationship. I'm surprised at Gary for not saying anything to her."

"I wasn't."

"Why? What else aren't you telling me, Carla?" She placed a finger under her partner's chin and forced Carla to look her in the eye.

"He's different. The accident has changed him. I know that's an obvious thing to say about someone lying in a hospital bed, but…"

"Give him time to get used to his injuries. Have the doctors given a prognosis yet?"

She nodded. "He'll probably walk again in six months. As for work, they're unclear about that as yet."

"Shit! Well, you're going to have to be patient with him then. That news would've come as a shock to him."

"I know that. Christ, I'm going to sound a right bitch now…it's the way he looks at me."

"Which is?"

"As though he hates me. As if he's reminded of the good times we had and like that is affecting the way he'll be in the future. I don't know. It makes no sense to me, so I'm willing to call it a day and stop wasting my energy on a man who clearly isn't interested in me."

Sara folded her arms and tapped her right foot. "I'm not here to criticise you, but hear me out. I think you'll regret making a hasty decision. Answer me this: how do you feel about him?"

"The truth is, I don't know. We've been together a few months. I'm not the type to fall head over heels in love with someone at the drop of a hat, unlike some I could mention."

"Don't go taking a swipe at me. I fell in love with Mark because he treated me right and we have such a lot in common."

"There you go then. Gary and I have very little in common except for the sex."

"Ah, that's what is at the crux of all this…you think the sex is going to dry up now due to the injuries he has sustained, right?"

Carla's head dropped again, and she sniffled. "Maybe."

"Oh, sweetie, I think it's natural for you to think along those lines. You're a young woman with needs, you're bound to want to put those needs first. I'm not going to lecture you about what is right and what's wrong as it's difficult to judge when you're not walking in someone else's shoes. All I can advise you to do is to hang in there. Don't for goodness' sake make any rash decisions that you're going to regret a few months or years further down the line."

Carla looked up at her, a trace of a smile spreading her lips apart. "How did you ever get to be so smart?"

Sara winked at her. "It's all in the genes. Now, do you want to stay with us or go home and get some rest? I'd rather you chose the latter. Either way, I don't mind; however, I need to get on. I've just come back from attending another murder scene."

"Oh crap. Can I stay? I promise if it gets too much for me, I'll give in and go home."

"On that proviso, welcome back into the fold." Sara hugged her. Carla let out a relieved breath against her ear. "You'll do the right thing in the end."

Carla pulled away and blew her nose on the toilet paper. "Right for him or for me?"

"For both of you. It's still early days, far too early to be making any major decisions either way."

"You're right. I suppose exhaustion heightens your sensitivity. That's what I'll put this slip down to."

"I would be inclined to do that, too. I'll let you make yourself presentable and grab us both a coffee. See you soon. I think we're going to have a long day ahead of us."

"I'll be there in a sec."

Sara reached the door to hear her partner say, "Thanks for caring, it means a lot." She smiled and continued on her journey to the incident room with a spring in her step. "Morning, all. Let me get my priorities in order first, a well-earned coffee, and then I'll fill you in on the incident I attended early this morning."

Sara collected two cups of coffee from the machine.

"Are things that bad, boss?" Jill asked, gesturing towards the cups she was holding.

"They're not both for me." She nodded at the door as Carla stepped through it.

"Welcome back," Jill shouted.

"Thanks, guys. Please, don't make a fuss." Carla walked over to her desk and sat in her chair.

Sara placed her cup of coffee in front of her partner. "Drink this. You're going to need it after what I tell you."

"Thanks. I could always change my mind and go home."

Sara laughed. She put on her serious face and told the team about the body that was discovered in the field earlier. "As you can imagine, there was no form of ID on this chap. I'd put his age around the mid-to-late forties."

"The same age as the other cases we're dealing with," Barry suggested.

"Seems that way. So that's three murders on our patch in the space of a few days."

"Do you want us to treat each case individually?" Carla asked, taking a sip from her cup.

"For now, I think we should. Although, Jill found a connection between Jensen and Annibal. Their wives apparently know each other through Facebook. Damn, I wish I'd taken a photo of this morning's victim on my phone."

"Lorraine will issue one eventually. Where do we go from here?" Carla asked.

"I need you guys to keep digging into the first two victims' backgrounds for now. We're looking for a connection between the two men. Frustratingly, nothing has shown up yet, apart from the fact that the two wives, or should I say one wife and one ex-wife, knew each other."

"What happens if we can't find anything?" Carla asked.

Sara threw her arms out to the side and let them slap against her thighs. "I haven't got a Scooby Doo. I'm going to tackle the usual in my office and then get on the blower to the lab. I hope to have something useful to add to the mix for you all soon. Don't forget, we're also trying to find a possible link to the IRA. How that might manifest is anybody's guess at this time. Keep an open mind, guys."

Carla seemed shocked by the news.

"The others will fill you in about victim two, it's a doozy." Sara rushed into her office to sort through the stack of mail she knew would be awaiting her.

After hearing nothing from Lorraine an hour later, she rang the lab.

"Jeez…you're getting impatient in your old age, Sara Ramsey. Give me a chance, we only returned from the scene half an hour ago."

"Sorry. Well, we're up in the air on all three murders. You can imagine what that's doing to the team's morale at this end."

"It's frustrating as hell for me and my team as well, you know. Give me another hour. I'll run the tests myself, how about that?"

"You're a legend."

"Ha…do you think they'll put that on my tombstone?"

"Words to that effect," Sara said, laughing as she ended the call. She left the office and visited each team member to see if there was anything new.

"I was just going to come and see you, boss." Jill said. "Working on the Facebook angle, I've pulled up the photos on both women's pages in the hope you might be able to recognise someone. There are a few group photos, functions or parties that may be of interest."

"Great idea." Sara collected a chair from the next desk and sat close to Jill.

Jill clicked on numerous photos, but no one grabbed Sara's attention.

"Nothing?" Jill asked.

"Wait. Hang on, can you highlight that one and possibly enlarge it?" Sara peered at the monitor and scratched the side of her head.

"I'll do my best." Jill worked her magic, and suddenly the man whose body had been discovered in the field a few hours earlier was sitting on the monitor, staring back at them.

Sara slapped her flattened hand on the desk and dropped back in her chair. "Bloody hell. There he is. I'm sure of it. I'll have to wait for

Lorraine to send the photos through, but to me, that's him. I'm ninety-nine percent positive."

"Excellent news. I'll print off a copy so we can add it to the board."

"Are any of the photos tagged with names?" Sara asked, her mind racing.

"Let me dig around, see what I can find out for you. I'll get back to you soon, boss."

Sara nodded and ran into her office when the phone rang. "DI Ramsey. How can I help?"

"It's me. This is going to cost you dinner."

Sara's heart raced at the sound of Lorraine's voice. "If I must. What have you got for me?"

"The victim is in the system for drink-driving offences, a warning and a conviction, dating back ten years."

"Get on with it, Lorraine."

"Bloody hell, you piss me off at times. He's Alan Beard. That's all I can give you."

"I could kiss you." Sara blew several kisses into the phone in her excitement.

"People will begin to talk if you carry on doing things like that, Ms Ramsey."

"Let them. This is the best news I've had all day. Thanks for getting back to me so quickly, I truly appreciate it. Pick a restaurant and a suitable time, and I'll see to the tab."

"That's a deal. Right, toodle-pip for now. I have a PM to perform. I'll send the report over as and when I've typed it up."

"Thanks, Lorraine. Speak soon."

"No doubt. I just hope we don't meet up at another murder scene any time soon."

"Agreed." Sara ended the call and leapt out of her chair. "We've got a name. Alan Beard. Get digging, guys. Source his address ASAP, and Carla and I will pay the family a visit."

"That was quick. How did Lorraine manage that?" Carla replied.

"Luckily for us, he was in the system for drink-driving offences."

"I have an address for you, boss," Christine shouted, beaming.

"Brilliant news. Carla, I presumed you'd want to come with me. If not, I can get Craig to tag along for the ride."

"I'm okay. I'm up for this."

"Get your jacket then." Sara darted back into her office, slipped on her three-quarter-length woollen coat and returned to the incident room.

She and Carla left the station and arrived at the Beard's residence around fifteen minutes later. The house was impressive and set back from the other houses on the exclusive cul-de-sac. It was nowhere near as large as the other two victims' houses, though. "Nice, but nothing in comparison to the others."

"Does that matter? Maybe they've fallen on hard times over the years and had to start over for some reason," Carla suggested.

"True enough. Never judge a book and all that. Let's go break the news."

They left the car and walked up the wide path, bordered on either side by cottage planting.

"Someone cares well for their garden," Sara said.

"Either that or they pay a gardener to look after it."

"Maybe."

Sara rang the bell and waited. Not long after, a smartly dressed woman in her early forties opened the door. Her short blonde hair appeared dishevelled, and she smoothed it down with her beautifully manicured fingers.

"Hello, Mrs Beard?"

"That's right, and you are?"

Sara and Carla showed their IDs. "DI Sara Ramsey and DS Carla Jameson. Would it be convenient for you if we came in for a chat?"

"Can you tell me what this is about first?"

To Sara's well-trained eye, the woman seemed agitated about something. "Is everything all right, Mrs Beard?"

"Yes, why? Sorry, it's not often you get the police knocking on your door. I'm a little nervous."

"May I ask why?" Sara prompted.

She shrugged. "I was asleep on the couch. Please forgive me, I don't know what I'm saying."

"Are you on some kind of medication which knocks you out during the day, Mrs Beard?"

"I wish. No, I've been up most of the night, worried."

"Can we come in?" Sara asked a second time.

"Sorry, of course. Excuse my dithering state. I'll make us some coffee. Come through to the kitchen."

They followed her through the expansive interior that had been disguised well by the exterior. *Why was that? To deter burglars perhaps?*

"Will instant do? I can't be bothered to get the proper coffee machine out and clean it up afterwards. I'm not in the right frame of mind for such boring jobs."

"Instant will do for us, it's what we're used to drinking during the day." Sara watched the woman make several mistakes during the coffee-making process. "Do you want me to do it?"

"No. I'm fine. Thanks." Once Mrs Beard had managed to place the boiling water in the three mugs without any more mishaps, she invited them to take a seat at the stark white table in the corner of the kitchen-diner which ran the length of the back of the house. The garden was larger than average and full of colourful plants and appeared to have been expertly landscaped. It included several seating areas and a pergola walkway through the middle of the lawn, covered by an abundance of differently coloured roses.

"Thanks for the drinks, much appreciated. We can never get enough coffee down our necks during the day." Sara smiled, trying to put the woman at ease.

"I tend to overdo the caffeine. I know it's not good for you, but it's addictive and steadies the nerves, doesn't it?" She offered a weak smile.

"Is there something wrong, Mrs Beard?"

She stared down at her coffee and nodded. "My husband didn't come home last night. I've tried ringing him, but nothing."

"Is he prone to disappearing?"

"No. He regularly stays away on business trips but usually keeps in contact with me during the course of the evening. I don't know where to turn next."

Sara sighed. "I'm sorry to have to tell you, Mrs Beard, but I believe your husband was murdered last night."

Her head slowly rose, and tears swelled in her eyes. "What?" The single word came out as a whisper.

"That's right. His body was found in a field on the main Worcester road this morning by a farmer at first light."

She placed her arm on the table and lowered her head onto it. "No. It can't be true. Not Alan, not my Alan. He can't be gone. What will I do without him? I won't survive...I can't..." Mrs Beard bawled for the next few minutes.

Sara and Carla let her, what else could they do? Sara glanced around at some of the photos placed on the furniture and on a few of the walls. Yes, it was definitely Alan who was their latest victim. Finally, Sara said, "Sorry, I don't know your Christian name."

"It's Jacqueline."

"Jacqueline, I'm sorry, I know this news must have come as a huge shock. Maybe we could ring a relative to be with you."

"Would you? Yes. That would be good. My sister. I'll get you her number." She left the table on wobbly legs and picked up the phone sitting by the back door on the worktop. "It's ringing," she said, returning to the table. Jacqueline put the phone on speaker.

"Hi, Jack, what's up?"

"Oh, Keely. Please, please, you have to come and be with me." Jacqueline broke down again.

"Hello, Keely..." Sara said.

"What? Who the hell is this? What have you done to my sister?"

"Please, calm down. I'm DI Sara Ramsey. I'm with the West Mercia Police. Your sister has received some very upsetting news about her husband. Is it possible for you to come over here to give her some support?"

"What type of news? Has he been involved in an accident?"

"Please, it would be better if we told you in person."

"I'll be right there. Jacqueline, stay strong, I'm coming, sweetheart."

"Thank you," Jacqueline croaked.

Sara pressed the End Call on the phone and set it to one side. "Does Keely live very far?"

"No, only round the corner. She should be here soon. Oh God, I want to know how he died but I'm afraid to ask."

"Why don't we wait until your sister gets here before we go into detail?"

Jacqueline nodded and fell silent, lost in a world of her own. The front door opened a few minutes into the silence, and a redhead, dressed in jeans and a thick jumper, came tearing into the kitchen.

Jacqueline left her chair and flew into her sister's arms. "Oh, love. What in God's name is going on?"

Jacqueline hugged her sister and mumbled, "He's dead, Keely. Alan is dead."

"No. This can't be true. Not Alan." Keely turned to face Sara and Carla and demanded, "How did this happen? Was it a car crash?"

"Why don't you both take a seat?"

The sisters, holding hands tightly, slipped into two of the chairs, in between Sara and Carla.

"Okay, now tell us." Keely insisted.

Sara sucked in a large breath then let it out slowly. "It would appear that Mr Beard was murdered last night and dumped in a field close to the main Worcester road." Sara paused for her sister's reaction to the news.

"What? Murdered? That type of thing doesn't happen around here, surely?"

"I'm afraid it does. At present, we're dealing with three deaths, men of a similar age to Alan. I know I'm asking a lot, Jacqueline, but are you up to answering some questions?"

"I'll try my best." Her hands left her sister's and grasped her coffee mug which she raised to her lips to take a sip of the cooling liquid.

"What type of questions? Is it really necessary when you've just delivered such devastating news?" Keely interjected.

"It is if we hope to catch the killer. I'm sorry if it causes you any discomfort, Jacqueline."

"I'm okay. I'll answer if I can."

"Perhaps we can start by trying to ascertain where your husband was yesterday evening?"

Agitated, Jacqueline ran a hand over her face. "Out."

"Out where?" Sara pushed gently.

"I don't know. I think he mentioned he had a business meeting to attend, but don't quote me on that."

Great, well, that's super helpful, thanks! "May I ask what line of business he's in?"

"Exports and imports. Based in Bristol."

"Would you mind giving us the details of where the business is based? We'll chase up his itinerary with his secretary if you can't fill us in," Sara said.

"I'll jot down the details for you," Keely said, reaching for Carla's notebook and pen. She scribbled an address at the Bristol Docks and passed it to Carla.

Sara nodded for Carla to get on to the station. Her partner left the room to make the call.

"Did he hold many business meetings in the evening?" Sara asked.

"Not many. Enough, though," Jacqueline replied, her attention never leaving the mug in her hands.

"Don't you guys rely on CCTV footage for a lot of your investigations?" Keely enquired.

"Most of the time, yes. We need to have a rough idea where the incident took place first, though."

Keely nodded and smiled as if to say 'that was a dumb question'.

"I'd like you to think over anything that has happened in the past few months, Jacqueline. Has your husband been on the end of any possible dodgy dealings that could have brought trouble to his door?"

"No, never. He was a law-abiding citizen."

Sara tilted her head. "He was convicted of drink-driving in the past, were you aware of that?"

"Of course I was," Jacqueline retorted sharply. "Sorry, I didn't mean for that to come out nasty. I'm upset."

"There's no need for you to apologise. Did he discuss his business with you?"

"No, not really. He brought in the money, and I spent it. Isn't that how most marriages work?"

"Maybe some do. Mine didn't." Sara bit her lip. She barely discussed her marriage at work amongst her colleagues, let alone with a total stranger.

"I apologise, I feel bad opening my mouth now."

"Don't feel bad, if that's how you feel. Perhaps you've noticed someone hanging around the house over the past week or so?"

Jacqueline glanced at her sister and shrugged. "No, I haven't. Have you when you've dropped over?"

Keely stared at her sister and shook her head. "Nope."

"We're going to need to delve into your husband's business in that case. Exports you say? Could he have possibly got into bed with the wrong type of people? Is that possible? People expecting him to smuggle illegal immigrants perhaps?"

Jacqueline's eyes widened. "Oh gosh, yes, I never thought about that. Oh, Alan, why did you do that?"

Sara raised a hand in front of her. "Let's not get too carried away with that notion. It was only a suggestion at this stage. One last question if I may, and then we'll leave you in peace."

"Of course. Fire away," Jacqueline said, a wary smile twitching on her lips.

"We're dealing with a few other cases that have come to our attention this week. Two men around Alan's age have also been found murdered. My wayward thoughts at the moment are possibly linking the men in some way. Maybe there's a connection we've yet to discover, who knows?"

"I see. How can I help?"

Sara chewed her lip for a second or two. "It's our job to check people's social media accounts nowadays during an investigation, and something prominent stuck out before we came over here today."

Jacqueline frowned. "Is that some kind of riddle? I don't understand what you're getting at, Inspector."

"Bear with me… Sorry, sometimes I'm prone to going around the houses. My partner will attest to that." She saw Carla nod out the corner of her eye. "What I was wondering is if your husband knew these other two men."

"What? I haven't got a clue what you're talking about," Jacqueline blasted defensively.

Sara raised a pointed finger. "I did say bear with me. I'll give you the men's names: Lens Jensen and Jack Annibal." She watched the red highlights in Jacqueline's cheeks disappear. Her head shook, and she seemed stunned by the news. Sara let the silence fill the room before she prompted, "Mrs Beard?"

Jacqueline swallowed. "Umm…you've floored me, I hadn't heard of their deaths. Oh God, I need to ring Mie and Maria to see how they're coping."

"You can do that in a moment, after we've gone." Something wasn't sitting right with Sara about the woman's reaction to the news.

"I don't have anything to say apart from they're friends of ours."

"Good friends?" Obviously they were, if their Facebook photos were anything to go by.

"I suppose you'd call us that."

"Okay, that's all for now. We'll get back to the station and begin the investigation. Here's my card. If either of you think of anything that might be useful to us, please don't hesitate to contact us." She slid a business card across the table and stood.

Carla tucked her notebook in her jacket pocket and followed Jacqueline and Sara back to the main door of the house.

Jacqueline held open the door. "Please, find whoever did this to my husband."

"You have my word we'll do our best."

Sara didn't speak again until they were back in the car. "What did you make of that?"

"Meaning? What, you think it was all an act?"

Sara chomped on the inside of her cheek and stared at the grand house. "That's my gut feeling, yes. She almost freaked out when I mentioned there was a connection to the other men."

"Can't say I noticed that. Are you sure you're not reading more into it? Of course, I might be guilty of feeling a little rusty what with having no kip the last couple of days."

Sara switched the engine on and drew away slowly on the gravelled driveway. "There's something there. I say we go back and dig even deeper into all of their backgrounds. I'll leave you with this thought: she said they were good friends and yet she wasn't aware of the other men's deaths. Sounds mighty suspicious to me."

"If you put it like that, then yes, you're spot on. We need more to go on than just your gut feeling, though."

Sara stopped at the exit of the drive and turned to face her partner. "No shit, Sherlock!"

12

----

*J*acqueline had to fake a migraine, and needing a lie-down, to get rid of Keely. Not that she didn't appreciate her sister helping her with her supposed grief. The second Keely left the house, Jacqueline rang Mie.

"Shit! The cops were here."

"Okay, take a breath. What did they say?"

"It was about Alan. They told me they'd found his body in a field this morning."

"Right. And how do you feel about that?"

"I'm okay. Good riddance, and I'll put the flags out later and all that. Mie, that's not why I'm ringing you. We need to call a meeting. I have something to tell all the girls."

"Such as?"

"I'll tell you all together. Ring them and organise a meet. I'm on my way over there now."

"When did the cops leave?"

"Around ten minutes ago. Why?"

"Just a thought. If you're anxious about something they've said but not willing to divulge what that is right now, you're going to need to calm down and think things through thoroughly. There's a possibility they could be watching the house—watching you, to be more specific."

"Bugger, I never thought of that. Okay, what are you suggesting?"

"I'll get the girls to gather at my house for lunch. Will twelve-thirty do you?"

"Yes, if you insist this is the right thing to do? I'm scared, Mie. Bricking it."

"Tell me what's wrong? I can help. Maybe I can put something into action this morning before we meet up."

"No, that's impossible. I'd rather tell you all at the same time. See you later." Mie didn't get the opportunity to hound her further because she hung up on her.

Jacqueline sat at the kitchen table, contemplating what her life was going to be like in the future when it suddenly dawned on her that she'd have to tell their daughter, Dana, that her father was dead. Dana still lived with them. She was twenty but spent a few nights a week at her boyfriend's house in Worcester; she was due back today around fourish. Jacqueline had plenty of time to get her emotions organised before her daughter arrived. She had a luncheon to attend first. Going upstairs, she ran a bath; she needed to soak her anxieties away.

Feeling more relaxed than she had done in quite a while, after her soak and dressing in a smart trouser suit, Jacqueline headed off for Mie's house. She was the second person to arrive. Maria, who was looking pretty sheepish, was already there, drowning her sorrows at the bar with a bottle of Prosecco sitting beside her. Jacqueline kissed Mie and Maria—the atmosphere in the room was noticeable. Mie did her best to be the hostess with the mostest, but even her usual bubbly nature failed to make an impact.

Di was the last to arrive. She was out of breath when she joined the others in the lounge. "Who called the meeting and why?"

"I did. Well, that's not quite true, I asked Mie to call it on my behalf," Jacqueline piped up.

"And? Why? What's going on?" Di challenged.

Jacqueline picked up her glass and crossed the room to stand by the open bi-fold doors. The sun was peeping through a cloud, basking her in its warmth. She raised her head and closed her eyes.

"Jesus, we're not here so you can top up your damn tan, Jackie. If you've got something to say, bloody spit it out," Mie yelled, her irritation clearly visible.

Jacqueline took a sip of her drink and turned to face the other three women. "They know."

"Who knows?" Mie asked, taking a step towards her.

Jacqueline swallowed noisily. "The police."

The other three women all stared at each other, their mouths gaping.

"How?" Mie eventually asked. "Did you open your damn mouth?"

Di stood between the angry Mie and Jacqueline. "Before anyone says or does something they regret, why don't you explain fully what you mean, Jacqueline? By fully I mean talking in complete sentences, not giving us the facts in dribs and drabs."

"Getting ratty with me isn't going to help…just saying, Di." Tears pricked her eyes. She was feeling emotional again, not because of the loss of Alan, no, because her friends appeared to be turning on her.

"I wasn't aware that I was getting ratty. Get on with it, Jacqueline, some of us have places we need to be."

Jacqueline glared at her. "Very well. The police have realised there's a connection between the murders. There, I've said it."

"What? How? What did they actually say? Word for word," Mie demanded.

"I can't remember word for word. The conversation went along the lines that there had been two other deaths of wealthy businessmen in the area this week and looking on social media it would appear that there is a connection."

"Shit! Social media…our fucking photos. Why didn't we frigging think to unfriend ourselves?" Di hissed through gritted teeth and paced a small area.

"Chill, will you? What's done is done. This doesn't mean anything," Mie said.

"Are you crazy?" Maria shouted, finally finding her voice after days of neglecting to show up.

"No one is crazy," Mie reprimanded her.

Maria growled. "There's a connection between us all. They'd have to be the bloody Keystone Cops not to figure out what's going on."

"I agree," Di said, stopping in her tracks in front of Jacqueline. She grabbed the collar of Jacqueline's blouse and pulled her to within inches of her face. "You'd better hold up your end of the bargain, bitch, otherwise…"

Mie rushed to Jacqueline's aid and unlatched Di's hand. "Pack it in. She'll do what's necessary, won't you, Jackie?"

Jacqueline's pulse raced, and a ripple of fear stroked the length of her spine. "I can't do it. Not now, it's too risky."

"What? You can't do it, or you *won't*?" Di screeched, attempting to swipe her around the face.

"Mie, you understand, don't you? If I do anything now, it's going to look bloody obvious what's going on," Jacqueline pleaded.

"What were the police like? Male or female?" Mie asked, her brow furrowed in concern.

"Two females. Does it frigging matter?" Jacqueline responded, sinking onto the edge of the sofa.

"Women are far more intuitive than men, in my opinion. Damn, this has all got out of hand. Di, I think Jackie is right, we need to put the pact on hold until the heat dies down."

Di jabbed Mie in the chest with her pointed finger. "That is not what I fucking signed up for, none of us did. She's been crapping herself since the first murder happened, haven't you, Jacqueline?"

Jacqueline stared at the floor, unable to look at her friends.

"See. She's too cowardly to admit it." Di unexpectedly punched Jacqueline in the head. "I ain't going to sit back and let her get away with this."

"What the fuck was that for?" Jacqueline rubbed her head.

"Calm down, Di. Jackie won't let us down, will you, Jack?"

Jacqueline's gaze rose to Mie, and she nodded. "I'm going to have to. I'm sorry, this has gone too far already. I can't be a part of this now."

Di reached out and yanked Jacqueline's head back. She smashed her fist into her face, missing her nose by inches when Jacqueline pre-empted what her friend was about to do and turned her head to the side.

Mie stamped her foot. "Ladies, control yourselves. Squabbling and fighting amongst ourselves isn't going to flipping help, is it?"

Maria coughed. "I knew this was a bloody mistake. I feel the same way Jacqueline does. We should call a halt to things now, with the view to possibly revisiting things once they've died down. If the police have uncovered a connection, surely, all we have to do is pretend they were connected through their businesses. How, I have no idea."

Mie nodded. "She's right. We need to think up a plausible excuse. They're obviously aware that we're all Facebook friends. It would be conceivable that the men might want a piece of the action in a deal that is worth millions. If the police start asking questions, we'll say it was a secret deal which none of us were privy to. Agreed?"

Jacqueline, Di and Maria remained thoughtful but silent for the next few minutes.

"It could work," Maria agreed.

"Damn right it could," Mie replied, beaming at her idea.

"I'm not so sure," Di said, glaring at Jacqueline. "I hate the thought that one of us has been let off the hook. We made a pact. Something that would join us together forever. There's a link missing. I know we're talking about my husband getting away with it, and maybe that's what is ticking me off so much." She threw an arm up in the air and paced again. "I feel cheated. You all have your freedom, and I'm still stuck in a dead-end marriage with a man I can't bear to be in the same room with, let alone sleep alongside."

"We're only asking you to have some patience for a few weeks, no more than that, Di, until things cool off with the police," Mie suggested.

"And if it doesn't? And the police come knocking on our doors and haul our arses into custody, what then?"

"Then it won't bloody matter, will it?" Jacqueline snapped back.

"Why you…if I get my hands on you…" Di shouted, trying desperately to grab Jacqueline's hair.

Mie intervened. "Pack it in. Threats like that aren't going to help, Di."

"They may not help, but it gets my point across. I'm warning you, Jacqueline Beard, if you go back on our deal, you're going to frigging regret it, take my word for that."

Jacqueline shook her head, tears pricking at her eyes as she rose to her feet. "All I can do is apologise, Di. I have to go now. Dana is due back later, and I have to figure out how I'm going to tell my baby that the father she adores isn't going to come home tonight, or ever again."

"When is she back?" Mie asked.

"She's catching the three thirty-two from Worcester Shrub Hill Station. She's due to get in around four-fifteen. I'm going to pick her up from the station. I have to go. I'm sorry things are fraught between us. I hope things settle down in the next day or two. If the cops come knocking on my door again, I'll tell them about the secret deal the men had and suggest you all do the same." She hugged Mie and Maria.

They returned her hug and pecked her on the cheek. However, when she approached Di, her dearest friend glowered at her and took a step back.

"I'm sorry, Di. I hope we'll be able to get past this in the future."

Di's eyes narrowed. "I doubt it, bitch." She turned to face the garden.

Mortified, Jacqueline left the house and rushed home again. She spent the rest of the afternoon soul-searching. She'd let her friends down, she realised that. How she could overcome such betrayal, well, that was the part she was struggling with. She decided to prepare Dana's special meal of homemade lasagne. Halfway through her task, it dawned on her that her daughter would probably be too distraught to eat it. She decided to finish the dish off anyway. It could go in the freezer if her daughter turned around and told her to stick her meal where the sun didn't shine. Dana was like that. Moody and often flew off the handle around that time of the month. She was all too aware they had spoiled her over the years. Given in to her demands when other kids in her year at school had been forced to earn their pocket money to buy the things they craved.

But deep down, her daughter was a kind and compassionate child. How she would react to the news was anybody's guess.

Jacqueline glanced up at the clock; almost three. Her daughter would be badgering her boyfriend to give her a lift to the station now, knowing Dana.

Jacqueline put the lasagne in the oven and poured herself a coffee. She sat at the table and watched the hands on the clock slowly work their way around until she picked up her car keys and set off for the train station at four o'clock on the dot.

She arrived in good time and waited for the passengers to come out of the entrance. The train pulled in a minute later. A mixture of excitement and trepidation grew within. She sat forward in her seat, peering over the steering wheel, surprised that Dana wasn't the first to appear, like she usually did.

The throng of people died down, and still no Dana. She got out of the car and rushed to the entrance, peering through the opening to the platform beyond. Nothing, no Dana. Rushing back to her car, she withdrew her mobile and punched in her daughter's number. It rang and rang until finally it was answered.

"Dana, where are you? I'm here waiting for you. The least you could do was ring me to tell me that you'd changed your mind and was staying there with Taylor."

"God, don't you ever come up for breath, bitch?"

Jacqueline's eyes darted around the area in front of her then closed as the comprehension sank in. "Di? Is that you?"

"Di, is that you?" her friend mimicked nastily. "Yes, it's me. If you want to see Dana again, you're going to uphold your end of the pact. Got that?"

"No!" Jacqueline screamed. Tears mixed with the snot running down her face as the devastation of what was happening took hold. "Please, Di, I can't do it."

"Then say goodbye to your daughter."

"Mum, what's she talking about? Help..." her daughter's voice sounded in the background, followed by a deafening slap.

13

Sara was sitting in her office when the phone rang. "DI Ramsey. How can I help?"

"Please, please, you have to help me. She's got my daughter..." The woman broke down in tears.

Sara recognised the voice but struggled to find a name. "Sorry, who is this?"

The woman sniffled and whispered, "Jacqueline Beard. Please come quickly."

"Okay, you need to tell me what's going on first, Jacqueline. You say someone has your daughter. How do you know this?"

"A phone call...please, if you come, I'll explain everything. We've...please, just come."

"We've what? What have you done, Jacqueline?"

"Not over the phone. Please, we're wasting time. My daughter's life is in danger. She has her..."

"Who has her?"

"Please, come."

Sara stood and hitched her jacket on. "All right, I'm on my way. Are you at home?"

"Yes, hurry, please."

"I'll be there soon. Don't do anything until I get there, you hear me?"

The line went dead.

Sara ran into the incident room. "I've just received an urgent call from Jacqueline Beard. Someone, a *she*, has kidnapped her daughter. That's all I could get out of her, except she told me that she would tell me everything when I arrived. Carla, are you feeling well enough to accompany me?"

"Too bloody right, try and stop me."

"Good. I need the rest of you to stay here. This could be the piece that pulls all this together. We're going to need to act on the information as soon as we get to hear what that is. We'll be in touch soon."

*S*ara and Carla arrived back at Jacqueline's mansion, with the aid of the siren, within five minutes. "Crap, you nearly caught that car. I thought we were goners there for a minute."

"Stupid idiot. Are you telling me he didn't hear us coming? I'm sure some motorists deliberately hamper a speeding cop car."

"You're probably right." Carla pointed at the front door of the house when Sara entered the drive. "We have a welcoming committee."

Sara drew the car to a halt next to Jacqueline's, and she and Carla jumped out and ran towards the house.

"Please, I'm going out of my mind with worry," Jacqueline pleaded, her hands clutched together as if in prayer.

"Let's go inside." Sara wrapped an arm around her shoulders and guided her back inside. "In the kitchen?"

"No, in here." She pointed at the first reception room off the hallway.

The lounge was larger than Sara was expecting. It had an accent wall of gold and brown high-gloss wallpaper. The rest of the room was painted in a subtle coffee colour.

They all took a seat. Sara sat next to Jacqueline on one of the couches while Carla took notes from the other.

"Now, why don't you start from the beginning? Who do you think has kidnapped your daughter and why?"

"I know she has her, she rang me…" Her eyes sparkled with unshed tears. "You have to do something."

"I can't do anything until you tell me what all this is about, Jacqueline."

"Things have got out of control."

"What things? There's no way we can help you get your daughter back if you don't confide in us."

Her head lowered, and she sighed. "We had a pact."

Sara and Carla eyed one another with intrigue.

"What kind of pact?" Sara asked gently.

"The worst kind. Only, well, I couldn't go through with my part."

"The worst kind? You're going to have to give us more than that, Jacqueline."

"Murder. All right, it was all about murder." The dam burst, and she held her hands over her face, smothering the tears as they cascaded down her cheeks.

Sara's eyes widened as her words sank in. "As in, the murders of the three men we've found this week?"

"Yes. The husbands. They all deserved to die, even mine, but when it came to the crunch, I couldn't go through with it."

"Are you telling me you're supposed to kill someone's husband?" Sara urged, trying to get to the bottom of things quickly.

Jacqueline nodded. "Yes, I was supposed to kill Di Powell's husband…I can't do it. She's furious with me, and my daughter was due home today from Worcester. Di must have pounced on her at Shrub Hill Station. I can't let anything happen to her. Please, can you help me?"

Sara puffed out her cheeks. "Of course we can try and help. First, I need to know every detail about the pact."

"What? Now? But Dana's life is in danger."

"I know, which is why you need to give us all the facts. We'll get your daughter back, I promise you. Right now, we need to know what type of people we're up against here."

She released a long-suffering sigh. "Ordinary housewives whose husbands have cheated on them for years. Maria was divorced, granted, but Jack was still treating her terribly. She was shocked when she heard that Mie had got a terrorist involved. Everything started to unravel then. Things got worse when Maria found out that Jack's girlfriend was pregnant. That's when I began having doubts as well. I tried my best to talk the others out of it. But I ended up drunk, and Di left the house and killed Alan. What a mess it all is."

"I see. And now Di feels aggrieved that you won't kill her husband and is trying to force your hand by kidnapping your daughter, is that it?"

"Yes. That's correct. Throughout this project the women have all changed. I don't recognise some of them any more."

"I'm not surprised if they've turned into killers. What did Di say to you?"

"What do you mean? She's threatened me that if I don't kill Victor...well, she said if I want to see Dana alive that I should carry out my assignment."

"Of killing Victor?"

"Yes. I can't do it. You have to help me overcome this, please?"

"I need to have a chat with my partner first. We'll sort things out, I promise." Sara motioned for Carla to join her in the hallway. She closed the door to the lounge behind her. "Jesus, can you believe what we've just heard in there? I know I can't."

"What do you suggest we do about it? We need to find this Di, but how? She'll have gone into hiding now, surely."

"I'm guessing you're right there. We need to get on to the station. I want the other two women picked up in case she tries to involve them in the kidnapping. That way she'll be on her own and liable to slip up."

"I'll organise that now."

"Okay, I'll get back in there and see what else I can get out of her. What a frigging mess, right?"

"It's like something out of an Agatha Christie bloody novel. Women bumping off their husbands just for the sake of it." Carla shook her head and withdrew her mobile from her pocket.

As Sara entered the room, Jacqueline turned to face her. "Are you going to help me?"

Sara sat beside her and placed her hand over Jacqueline's. "Of course we're going to help you. I need you to be totally honest from here on, otherwise Dana's life could be in grave danger, especially as Di has already murdered your husband. It was a gruesome murder, too, I hasten to add."

Jacqueline broke down again. "Please, don't tell me that. I'll be honest, I swear, everything I've told you so far has been the truth. I just want my daughter back in one piece. She's already killed Alan, please, I'm begging you. You have to stop her before she kills Dana."

"We'll do our best to prevent that from happening. How well do you actually know this woman?"

"We've known each other for over ten years. We used to be really close, until all this blew up in our faces."

"What type of person is she? Usually stable? Happy-go-lucky? Moody? Violent? Aggressive?"

Jacqueline stared off in the distance as she contemplated her answer. "I suppose stable, but recently, yes, moody, unpredictable even. Oh God, why did I say that?"

"Let's work with stable for now and, for the moment, put aside that she has your daughter. Any idea where she's likely to take Dana? Does she have a favourite place where you all go perhaps?"

"I can't think of anything. My mind is in a muddle." Jacqueline pulled her hair by the roots.

Sara reached for her hand and covered it again with her own. "Remain calm. The only way you're going to get through this is if you do that."

"That's easy for you to say…I'm sorry, I shouldn't have snapped."

"Don't apologise. Try and think about a possible location."

"Would her house be too obvious?"

"Yes, we'll send someone to the house, but the likelihood of her being there is virtually zero. What about a second home, a holiday home perhaps?"

"I can't think of one. Maybe the others will know? No, I can't ask them, they'll sense something is going on, that the police are involved. Shit! Why can't I get my brain into gear? My daughter's life depends on me, and here I am concerned about what the other women will think about me."

Sara could tell she was hyperventilating. "Okay, breathe, nice and slowly. Controlled breaths in and out. Do it with me, Jacqueline. In... and out. Is that better?"

"Yes, I think so."

Carla came back into the room and nodded at Sara.

"What does that mean? Have you found her?" Jacqueline's head swivelled between them.

"No. We've instructed our team to be on the lookout for Di's vehicle, amongst other things."

"Other things?"

"All part of the investigation. I won't bore you with the details," Sara dodged nicely.

"What if the others find out I've involved the police? It was part of the pact not to. Bloody hell, they'll lynch me the first chance they get." Her hand shook as she brushed the stray hairs back from her face.

"They won't get the *chance*. They'll be in custody. We'll protect you."

"What? You're going to arrest the others...? What am I thinking? Of course you will. Me and my big mouth. All I'm trying to do is save my daughter's life, and in the process, I've opened a can of bloody worms."

"Please, don't be too hard on yourself, Jacqueline. There was no way any of you would get away with murder. Not nowadays. We were already on the trail; we had our suspicions about Mie and Maria anyway. You know that through the social media. Criminals need to be cagier these days. The truth is, most of them haven't got a clue how to truly deceive the detectives in an investigation."

Jacqueline stared at her, gobsmacked. "So the net was already closing in on us?"

"Yes. Nice and tight. Now that's out of the way, why don't you sit back and try to think about where Di might have taken Dana?"

Jacqueline did as she was instructed and continued to breathe deeply in and out as she thought.

Sara and Carla remained silent for the next few minutes until Jacqueline's eyes flew open and she bounced forward.

"I think I remember. A distant memory is telling me that Di and Victor bought one of those log cabins in the heart of the Forest of Dean. She hasn't mentioned it for a few years. I don't even know if she still owns it."

Sara shot out of her chair. "It's enough for us to be going on with." She left the room and dialled the station. Craig picked up. "Craig, I think I might have a possible hiding place. A log cabin in the Forest of Dean. Try and trace that for me, will you? Ring me back ASAP."

"Will do, boss. Just to bring you up to date on what else is going on, two arrests have been made: Mie Jensen and Maria Annibal. Our guys are bringing them in now."

"Good. Let them stew in a cell for a while. I'll question them later. Not that they'll be able to worm their way out of this one. We've got them by the short and curlies, there's no doubt about it."

"That's great news. I'll ring you when I can."

Sara ended the call and returned to the lounge. She grinned at Carla. Carla nodded her understanding.

"I can see you, you know. Please, any news yet on my daughter?" Jacqueline asked.

"No, it's too soon for that. Mie and Maria have both been arrested, so there's no chance of them helping Di escape, if that thought had crossed her mind."

"Shit! They're going to kill me when they find out."

"Nonsense. Now all we have to do is call Di. I propose that you pretend you're going to go along with your original plan."

"What? You want me to kill Victor?"

"I want you to tell her that's what you intend to do. It's the only way I can conceive getting your daughter back."

"Can't you go to the cabin? Storm it and release my daughter?"

"Yes, we'll do that. But if we do things my way, it'll put Di off the scent of suspecting anything is likely to go wrong. Does that make sense?"

Jacqueline ran a shaking hand over her face. "I think so. You're asking me to ring her and tell her I'm going to kill Victor."

"That's correct. Are you up to it?"

"I suppose I have to be if I want to get Dana back alive."

Sara nodded. "Make the call. Be strong."

"I'll try." Jacqueline picked up her mobile and dialled Di's number, then she put the phone on speaker.

"Hello? Come to your senses yet, have you?"

"Di, yes. I'll agree to kill Victor. Please don't hurt Dana."

"I won't. I never intended to do this. You forced my hand, Jackie. You did this, no one else."

"I'll do what I have to do. Tell me where and when?"

"Tonight. He'll be at home all evening, from around six. The sooner you do it, the quicker Dana will be back with you."

"I'll kill him. I won't let you down again."

"You'd better not…or else."

"I won't. Can I speak to Dana?"

"A quick word."

"Mum, what have you done? Don't do this. I'm begging you. What will happen to me if you go ahead and kill someone and get put into prison for it? Think seriously about this."

"Shut up, bitch. Sit down." Di came back on the line, sounding angry.

"Please, she's young and has her whole life ahead of her. Don't hurt her, Di. I'll do what you want. I'll get ready now. How do you want me to kill him?"

"For Christ's sake, you should've worked that out already. You'll be bloody wanting me to do my own dirty work soon."

"I'll figure something out. Is Dana all right? She knows about her father now, I suppose?"

"Yeah, I filled her in on every last detail to keep her in line. Enough of this. You have a murder to prepare for."

"No, wait. Once I've killed Victor, when will I get Dana back?"

"You'll get her back when I've seen photographic evidence that he's dead."

"What?"

"Just do it, Jackie. Prove to me you've got the guts to go through with this."

"I will. I'm going now. Don't hurt my daughter any more, I'm begging you."

Di ended the call.

Jacqueline set her phone down on the arm of the couch and sobbed. "I can't go through with this. I don't have the nerve..."

"You won't have to. We'll fake his death if we have to and send her the image. You've done the hard part by ringing her. Come on, Jacqueline, don't give up now. I'll come with you to see Victor. We'll explain what's happened. I'm sure he'll assist us."

"Oh God, do you think? What if he rings her and has a go at her?"

"He won't. I won't allow him to do that."

*H*alf an hour later, Sara and Carla drove Jacqueline to Victor's address. Sara had contacted the station en route to get an update from Craig. He informed her that he'd dispatched a team to search the woods for the cabin and was awaiting a call from the officers at the scene.

The three of them exited the vehicle and approached the house.

When Victor opened the door, he was clearly surprised to see them. "Can I help? Jacqueline? What are you doing here?"

Sara flashed her warrant card and introduced herself and Carla. "May we come in, Mr Powell?"

"For what? And why is she here?" he demanded, jutting his chin at Jacqueline.

"We'll explain inside," Sara stated, striding past the man into the hallway.

"Hey, I know my rights, and you can't come barging in here like this. Explain yourselves?"

"If you'll give me a chance, that's what I intend to do. Can we make ourselves comfortable in the lounge perhaps?"

"Do I have a choice?" He stormed across the large hallway and entered a huge lounge. "Sit down, if you must."

"Thank you. I'd advise you to do the same. We have something very unpleasant to tell you, sir."

Sara sat next to Jacqueline in case Victor flew at her once the reason behind their visit was revealed.

"I have my dinner in the oven. My wife is otherwise engaged this evening, and I'd rather not let it burn. So, say what you've got to say and get out."

"Why the hostility, sir?" Sara challenged.

"I'm sorry. I didn't mean to appear rude. It has been a fraught day at work, and I wasn't expecting to come home and cook for myself."

"Where is your wife?"

"Swanning around with one of her mates, I shouldn't wonder. Which brings me back to my question: why is she here?" he retorted heatedly, jabbing a finger in Jacqueline's direction.

"I have some regrettable news to share with you, sir. Please take a seat."

He huffed and threw himself into an armchair close to where he was standing. "There, now tell me."

"First of all, I need you to listen to me carefully and promise me that you will keep calm."

"I can't promise that if I don't know what you're going to tell me, can I?"

"You're not making this easy for me, sir. Here's the thing: your wife is currently on the run, and she's not alone."

His brow furrowed, and he shook his head a few times. "Sorry, what did you just say?"

"I know it's hard to believe. But, yes, your wife is on the run, and sadly, she's kidnapped Mrs Beard's daughter."

"Why? I don't understand any of this."

"This is where things get complicated, and I'm going to seek your help to pull this off."

"Pull what off? Get to the point, woman," he replied brusquely.

"Your wife is holding Dana Beard captive so Jacqueline will do something in return."

He motioned with his hand for Sara to get on with it. "And?"

"And Jacqueline has come here this evening to kill you."

"What in the blazes is that supposed to damn well mean? You're the police, aren't you?"

"We are, sir. We're here to ensure that neither you nor Jacqueline get hurt. However, we're going to need your cooperation to help us get Dana back unharmed."

"Me? What can I possibly do? You know my damn wife is going through the menopause, don't you? It's made her loopy. She keeps doing things that are totally out of character for her."

"Such as killing someone?"

"What? She hasn't?" His mouth dropped open.

"I'm afraid she killed Jacqueline's husband last night, and now your wife is expecting Jacqueline to return the favour and kill you."

"This is incomprehensible. Are you sure? Where's the evidence? How?"

"Petrol was involved, that's all I'm prepared to say in front of Mrs Beard."

He cupped his chin with his hand. "Our bloody bedroom stank of the stuff last night. When I tackled her about it, she told me she'd filled up the car and spilt some petrol on her trousers which she'd left in the corner of the room. I thought it odd at the time."

"Are you prepared to help us, sir? Time is getting on, and your wife will be getting impatient. There's no telling what she's likely to do to Dana if that happens."

"What are you expecting me to do?"

"Act dead."

"Are you crazy?"

"Not at all. You either act dead, or...I'll leave that to your imagination. Either way, your wife is expecting Jacqueline to send her a picture of your demise."

"This is ludicrous. Why don't you get out there and try and find her?"

"We're in the throes of doing that, sir. Will you help us?"

He sighed heavily. "If there's no other way, then I suppose I'll have to."

"Do you have any ketchup, or better still, red paint lying around?"

"No paint. In case you haven't noticed, the house is all white. I think there are some tinned tomatoes in the pantry, that'll do, won't it?"

Sara glanced at Carla. "Too red, isn't it?"

"Yep, we could add some brown sauce or balsamic vinegar to it, I suppose."

"Good idea. Can you organise that for me?"

Carla rose from her seat. "In the kitchen I take it, sir?"

Victor nodded. "Indeed. Just off the kitchen there's a door on the left."

"I'll find it."

Sara's phone rang. "Excuse me a second." Sara answered the call. "Craig, what have you got for me?"

"Boss, the cabin has been located. The guys at the scene say there's a light on inside."

"Excellent, hold on." She held the phone away and asked Victor, "Is there anyone using your cabin at present?"

"How do you know about that?"

"Just answer the question, sir."

"No. It should be empty, unless…could it be Di?"

"We think so. Do you both have a key to the place?"

"No, we only have one between us."

"Where do you keep it?"

He rushed out of the room and returned seconds later. "It's gone. She must have it."

"Thank you. That's all we need to know." She lifted the phone to her ear again. "Did you hear that, Craig?"

"Yes, boss. How do you want us to proceed?"

"Cautiously. She's killed before. There's no telling what she's capable of if we force her into a corner. Here's what I suggest…"

. . .

173

en minutes later, and the scene was set. Victor agreed to lie at an odd angle on the floor in the hallway. He'd sorted out a few essentials needed for them to fake his death. One of those items was a lump of Blu-Tack. Victor was wearing a three-piece suit, the waistcoat of which was a loose enough fit to hide the Blu-Tack beneath. Sara fetched a large knife from the kitchen and placed it through the opening between the buttons on the waistcoat and wedged the blade into the Blu-Tack. Then Carla placed the juice of the tomatoes on the tiles beside his head and mixed in some balsamic vinegar. The varying shades of red worked well, and they were pleased with their efforts.

"Okay, stay there, Victor. We're going to take several photos."

"Get on with it, my neck is killing me," he replied angrily.

Jacqueline gave Sara her phone. "There you go, perfect," Sara said after she shot off several photos. Jacqueline agreed. "Now you're going to have to ring her. Be brave, use your acting skills. I need you to come across as being triumphant and relieved that the murder has been committed. If she asks how you killed him, tell her you whacked him over the head several times and then thrust a knife into his chest."

Jacqueline practised her deep breathing technique to calm her nerves and then announced she was ready to make the call.

"Let's do this. Okay, you can get up now, sir. Carla, why don't you take Victor into the lounge? I'll stay here while Jacqueline makes the call."

Carla helped Victor to stand.

The knife fell away from his chest and dropped on the floor at his feet. "That was close." He grinned at Carla, and she stifled a chuckle.

Sara hugged Jacqueline. "I'll be right here with you. Let's send two photos first and then ring her."

Jacqueline did that and then swallowed as she rang the number. "Hi, it's me. Did you get the photos?"

"I did. Well done you. How do you feel?"

"Fine. It was a breeze. I bashed him on the head a few times then stuck the knife in his chest. Can I have my daughter back now?"

"Of course. I'm sorry it came to this. I wouldn't have hurt her. I'm bringing her home now."

Sara stepped away from Jacqueline, made the sign to cut the call short and got her own phone out ready. As soon as Jacqueline ended the call, she collapsed onto the floor.

Sara rang the station. "Craig, go, go, go."

"Hang on the line, boss. I have the officer in charge on the other phone."

"I'll wait." Covering the phone with her hand, she called out, "Jacqueline, are you all right?"

She looked up with tears bulging in her eyes. "I will be. Please, get my daughter away from her."

Sara heard Craig shouting down the line. "Craig, what's going on?"

"They've got her, boss. Dana is safe."

"Thank God. Good work. We'll be back soon." Sara hung up and got down on her knees next to Jacqueline who was sobbing. "Hush now. Your baby is safe."

"Thank you so much. How am I ever going to repay you?"

"This doesn't end here, Jacqueline. There will be consequences to pay for your actions, you realise that, don't you?"

"I know. I'm sorry for my part in all this. I truly am."

Sara helped her to her feet as Carla stepped out of the lounge. "What's going on?"

"She's safe. The officers have picked them both up."

"Thank God for that," Carla muttered.

You can say that again!

EPILOGUE

*T*hat night was exceptionally long. The interviews took place until the early hours of the morning. Sara gave an exhausted Carla her marching orders around midnight. Thankfully, she didn't kick up a fuss. Sara arrived home just after three in the morning. She fell asleep on the couch rather than wake Mark at such an ungodly hour. Thank God it was the weekend. She needed the next two days off to recuperate.

After spending the rest of Saturday sleeping, she and Mark set off for the planned barbeque at her parents' house on Sunday at twelve. Sara was relieved to see her sister there and she took Lesley to one side to ask how she was getting on with her unwelcome dilemma.

"I'm getting there. I had a surprise visit from the loan shark a few days ago."

Sara gasped. "You did? You should have called me."

"Actually, it would have been a waste of time. He was really nice about things once I explained what Brendan had done. He told me not to worry and that the debt remained with Brendan. He'll be seeking recompense from him in the future and not from me."

Sara hugged her sister. "That's fabulous news, sweetheart. Now you can live your life as it should be led, free from worry and excruciating debt. What about Brendan? Has he shipped out yet?"

"I helped him move the last of his stuff yesterday. As soon as he left the house, I arranged for someone to come in and change the locks. There's no way that bastard is getting back in my house. The deeds are due to be altered this week, which is a blessed relief. I've been so foolish." Her chin dropped onto her chest.

Sara placed a finger under it and tilted her sister's head back. "You'll find someone new, someone more deserving of your kind nature."

"We'll see. It's going to be difficult to trust anyone again after this disastrous relationship."

Sara hooked her arm through Lesley's and steered her back towards the rest of the family. "You will. Look at me, I found Mark when I was least expecting him to come along."

"Yeah, that's what I keep telling myself. Enough about me, we're all dying to hear about your latest investigation."

Mark topped up her glass of wine, and everyone took a seat at the table. Sara went through the crimes one by one without any one of them interrupting, except for the odd gasp.

At the end, her mother asked, "So what will happen now?"

"Three of the women will be charged with murder, and Jacqueline will have a lesser charge of accessory to murder thrown at her. What flummoxed me was that one of the women was already divorced, and another had set the wheels in motion and yet they still entered into that damned pact. Why put themselves through that? Why not let bygones be bygones and get on with their lives? Do these people seriously think that the police are useless idiots? Don't answer that, you lot, it was a rhetorical question."

They all laughed as Sara's mobile vibrated across the table.

"Sorry, it's Carla, I need to take this." She rushed to the other end of the garden and answered it. "Carla, is everything all right?"

"Stop worrying. Yes, everything is fine. I'm at the hospital now. Gary has had the best news ever."

"Which is?" Sara asked impatiently.

"The swelling has gone down, and he's up and walking around. Tentatively, but it's a start."

"That's terrific, love. I'm thrilled for you both. So no more doubts flashing through your mind then?"

"No. He sent his mother home. Apologised for not sticking up for me. Everything is as it should be between us and…" Carla paused for a few seconds.

"You can be an annoying bitch at times. Get on with it, woman. And?"

"And I might have accepted his proposal."

Sara screamed with joy. The rest of her family all turned to stare at her. She gave them a thumbs-up sign as tears ran down her cheeks. "Oh, Carla, I'm so thrilled for you both."

"Thanks. I'd better get back to my fiancé now. Ooo…that sounded funny."

Sara chuckled. "Hey, you'll get used to it. Okay, see you at work in the morning. We'll have a celebratory doughnut over a cup of coffee."

"Gee, you sure know how to celebrate the best things in life, don't ya?"

"I do indeed. Send Gary my congratulations."

"I will. Enjoy the rest of your day."

"You, too, Carla. Glad to hear you so happy."

"Thanks, Sara."

She ended the call and made her way back to the table where everyone was waiting to hear the news.

"Well?" her mother demanded eagerly.

"Carla just got engaged, isn't it wonderful? And Gary has been up and about. He's on the mend." Sara noticed a look pass between her mother and Mark and asked, "All right, you two, what's going on?"

Mark left his chair and knelt down on one knee beside her. "Carla's news is brilliant. Fancy making it a double wedding?" He produced a diamond and sapphire gold ring and slipped it on her shaking finger.

"Is this for real? Oh my goodness…of course I'll marry you."

Her father disappeared into the house and returned with a bottle of champagne and five glasses.

"You all knew?" she asked, shocked that her family had managed to keep it a secret from her.

"We did. Congratulations…to Sara and Mark. May you have many, many years of happiness ahead of you," her father toasted.

Sara noticed Lesley's head sink. She clutched her hand. "You'll find your prince charming one day, love."

"I'm delighted for you both, couldn't be happier."

Sara smiled and kissed her new fiancé on the lips. She raised a glass and chinked it against his. "To us."

"To us and the bright future ahead of us."

THE END

NOTE TO THE READER

Dear Reader,

Friends, you can't live with them and you can't live without them. Be careful of the pacts you create with them going forward, you never know where it might lead.

DI Sara Ramsey tackles one of her most gruesome crimes in the next book in the series, so don't miss the one, will you?

Grab your copy today of TWISTED REVENGE

Thank you as always for your support, if you wouldn't mind leaving a review, I'd be eternally grateful.

Happy reading

M A Comley

Made in the USA
Monee, IL
19 April 2022